THE ORDER
OF
GOOD THINGS

James M Fox

Copyright © 2026 James M Fox

All rights reserved.

No part of this publication may be reproduced, stored in a retrieval system, or transmitted in any form or by any means, electronic, mechanical, photocopying, recording, or otherwise, without the prior written permission of the author, except for brief quotations in reviews.

First edition: January 2026
ISBN (paperback): 979-8-9934194-0-4
ISBN (ebook): 979-8-9934194-1-1
theorderofgoodthings.com

SPECIAL THANKS

I want to give thanks to all of my current and previous Eagle brothers and sisters—thank you for your support. I dedicate this to the future Eagle members and hope that this story brings awareness and appreciation for live music and performers everywhere. Special Thanks to Phil Franks who hosts our Wednesday Open Mic at Folsom Eagles 929.

WITH GRATITUDE

I'm deeply grateful to my fellow Eagle members, whose camaraderie, curiosity, and steadfast spirit opened a new door into the rich history of our organization. Your stories, insights, and encouragement helped shape this project and grounded it in the legacy we share. This book is a tribute to that enduring spirit —where fellowship meets discovery, and the past finds new life through storytelling.

I also want to thank my family and friends for their thoughtful input, honest feedback, and unwavering support throughout this journey.

CONTENTS

1	THE ARRIVAL	1
2	THE MACHINE'S PROMISE	11
3	THE BOARDING HOUSE	29
4	MORAN SHIPYARD	45
5	JOURNEY SOUTH	65
6	THE GOLDEN EAGLE	83
7	SPREADING WINGS	99
8	THE POWERHOUSE	117

1

THE ARRIVAL

Seattle, Washington - February 1898

The Northern Pacific locomotive wheezed to a stop at Seattle's Union Station like a dying beast, steam hissing from its joints and coal smoke hanging thick in the February air. Daniel O'Malley pressed his face to the soot-stained window and felt his chest tighten at the sight before him. This wasn't the Seattle of his imagination.

The city sprawled before him in a chaos of mud and ambition. Hastily-built wooden structures crowded against brick buildings that rose from streets still unpaved from the great fire nine years prior. Everywhere, men moved with purpose—stevedores hauling cargo from ships, construction workers carrying lumber, and an endless stream of prospectors fresh from Alaska, their eyes wild with gold fever and their pockets heavy with dust.

"End of the line!" the conductor bellowed, his voice

cutting through the car's stale air. "Seattle! Gateway to the Klondike!"

Daniel clutched his violin case closer to his chest, the worn leather warm against his wool coat. Inside lay his most precious possession—a fiddle his grandfather had carried from County Cork forty years before. It had survived the crossing to America, poverty in Boston's Irish quarter, and now this journey west on the promise of work in the theaters and saloons of a boom-town drunk on gold rush money.

He shuffled down the narrow aisle with the other passengers, boots slipping on the ice-slick steps as he descended to the platform. The February cold bit through his threadbare coat, and the smell of the city hit him like a physical blow—sawdust and sewage, coal smoke and salt air, the metallic tang of money changing hands too quickly.

"Careful with them instruments!"

Daniel spun toward the sound, watching in horror as a burly railroad worker hefted a battered guitar case like a sack of grain. The case landed with a sickening crack against the platform boards.

"That's delicate!" Daniel called out, rushing forward. "Those are musical instruments, not freight!"

The worker, a thick-necked man with tobacco-stained whiskers, barely glanced up. "It's all freight to me, boy. You want it handled special, you pay special."

"But the music—"

1 THE ARRIVAL

"Music?" The man spat into the mud. "Hell, you musicians are gonna be out of work soon enough anyway." He jerked his thumb toward a wooden crate being unloaded from the baggage car. "See that? Edison's latest. One of them talking machines. Why pay you fiddle players when we got all the music we need in a little wax cylinder?"

Daniel stared at the crate, his stomach dropping. Even here, at the edge of the continent, the phonograph had arrived first.

"You hear me, Irish?" The worker tossed another instrument case, this one containing someone's banjo. "Machines don't need to eat. Don't need beds. Don't go on strike."

The word 'strike' hung in the cold air like a curse. Daniel had heard rumors back in Chicago—musicians in Seattle organizing, demanding better pay, fighting the theater owners who grew rich while performers scraped by. But seeing this man's casual cruelty, the mechanical crate sitting among the musical instruments like a coffin at a wedding, Daniel understood that the fight here was about more than money.

It was about whether music had a soul.

"Daniel? Daniel O'Malley?"

He turned to find a young woman approaching through the crowd. She was perhaps twenty-two, with auburn hair pinned up beneath a blue wool hat and eyes the color of stormy seas. Her dress was well made but practical, the kind worn by someone who worked for her living but took pride in her appearance.

"I'm Clara Weston," she said, extending a gloved hand. "Tommy Morrison said you might be on this train. He wrote ahead from Chicago—said you play fiddle like an angel and might be looking for work."

Daniel shook her hand, grateful for the human warmth after the railroad worker's coldness. "Miss Weston. Yes, I'm hoping to find regular work. Tommy said Seattle's got more theaters than it knows what to do with."

Clara's smile flickered. "It did. Before the—" She glanced around nervously, then lowered her voice. "Before the trouble started. Come on, let's get you out of this wind. I know a place where we can talk properly."

As they walked through the crowded streets, Daniel marveled at Seattle's raw energy. Every block seemed to contain a saloon, a hotel, or a storefront advertising passage to Alaska. Men in fur coats walked alongside others in rags, all united by the golden dreams that had drawn them north. The air rang with a dozen languages—English, Norwegian, Chinese, German—and underneath it all, the sound of construction as the city built itself around its sudden wealth.

"There," Clara pointed to a two-story building wedged between a hardware store and a shipping office. A painted sign read "Morrison's Music Hall - Live Entertainment Nightly." But the windows were dark, and a small notice was tacked to the door.

"What's that sign say?" Daniel asked, though he suspected he knew.

1 THE ARRIVAL

"'Closed due to labor dispute,'" Clara read aloud. "Same as half the theaters in town. The musicians are striking, and the owners are being stubborn as mules."

"What do they want? The musicians, I mean."

"Fair wages. Decent working conditions. Some assurance they won't be replaced by—" She nodded toward a nearby saloon, where the tinny sound of a phonograph drifted through the batwing doors. "By those things."

They passed the saloon, and Daniel could hear the mechanical reproduction of what might once have been a waltz, now reduced to scratchy approximation. Inside, he glimpsed men gathered around a wooden cabinet with a large horn protruding from its top, their faces lit by the yellow glow of gas lamps.

"Fascinating invention," a well-dressed man was saying to the crowd. "No musicians to pay. No temperamental performers. Just wind it up and let it play."

Daniel felt Clara tense beside him. "That's John Cort," she whispered. "One of the theater owners. He's been showing off that machine all week, making sure every musician in town sees it."

Through the window, Daniel watched Cort cranking a handle on the side of the Edison phonograph. The machine began its mechanical performance, and the men leaned closer, some nodding approvingly. Daniel felt a tightness in his chest, recognizing the eager faces of men who didn't yet understand what they were applauding

"The future of entertainment, gentlemen," Cort was saying. "Reliable. Affordable. No strikes, no demands, no —"

His words were interrupted by a commotion from the street. A group of men approached the saloon, their faces grim and their hands clenched into fists. Daniel recognized the calluses and careful posture of musicians—the way they protected their fingers, the alert way they listened to every sound around them.

"That's Billy Murphy and his boys," Clara said quietly. "They've been out of work for three weeks now."

The lead musician, a wiry man with prematurely gray hair, pushed through the saloon doors. The phonograph's waltz ground to a halt as he lifted the needle with deliberate care.

"Evening, Mr. Cort," Murphy said, his Irish accent thick with controlled anger. "Enjoying your mechanical orchestra?"

Cort straightened, his hand moving instinctively toward his vest pocket—perhaps where he kept a pistol, Daniel thought. "Evening, Billy. Just demonstrating the latest in modern convenience."

"Convenient, is it?" Murphy picked up one of the wax cylinders, examining it like a jeweler studying a flawed diamond. "Tell me, does this little tube know when to play soft for a lady's tears? Can it read a crowd and know when they need a drinking song versus a hymn? Does it feel the music, or just repeat it?"

1 THE ARRIVAL

The saloon had gone quiet except for the crackle of the fire and the distant sound of ships' horns from Elliott Bay. Daniel found himself holding his breath.

Cort's voice was steady but cold. "It does what I pay it to do, Billy. Without complaint. Without strikes. Without demanding I treat it like it's something more than hired help."

"Hired help," Murphy repeated, setting the cylinder down with exaggerated care. "Is that what we are to you?"

"You're employees. Nothing more, nothing less."

Murphy nodded slowly, then turned to address the entire saloon. "You hear that, boys? We're just employees. Replaceable as a burnt-out gas lamp." He gestured toward the phonograph. "This machine— it's the future, Mr. Cort says. No strikes, no demands."

He paused, letting his words sink in.

"But I'll tell you what this machine can't do. It can't look into a miner's eyes and know he needs to hear about home. It can't feel when a song should build or when it should whisper. It can't comfort a widow or celebrate a birth or send off the dead with the respect they deserve."

Murphy's voice was rising now, carrying the rhythm and passion of a natural performer. "Music isn't just sound, Mr. Cort. It's community. It's the thread that holds people together when everything else falls apart."

"Pretty words," Cort replied, but Daniel could hear

uncertainty creeping into his voice. "But pretty words don't fill theaters or pay bills."

"Neither does a machine that puts people out of work." Murphy gestured toward the crowd of men who'd followed him into the saloon. "Every musician you replace with that contraption is a customer who can't afford your whiskey anymore. Every family that loses its income is ten people who won't be coming to your shows."

For a moment, the two men stared at each other across the smoky room. Daniel felt the weight of history pressing down on them all—the old world of live performance meeting the new world of mechanical reproduction, tradition facing progress, human souls confronting the relentless march of technology.

Then Cort reached over and wound the phonograph again. The waltz resumed its tinny performance, and he smiled coldly at Murphy.

"The future doesn't negotiate, Billy. It just arrives."

Murphy nodded once, as if he'd expected nothing else. "Then I guess we'll have to make our own future." He turned to his fellow musicians. "Come on, boys. We've got work to do."

As the musicians filed out of the saloon, Clara tugged at Daniel's sleeve. "We should go," she whispered. "This isn't over, and it's going to get uglier before it gets better."

They walked quickly through the gathering darkness, their breath visible in the cold air. Around them, Seattle

1 THE ARRIVAL

pulsed with its relentless energy—construction hammers echoing off the hills, ships' whistles calling from the harbor, the distant sound of music drifting from those few establishments still open.

"Where am I going to stay?" Daniel asked as they approached a modest boarding house on Second Avenue. "And where will I find work if the theaters are all closed?"

Clara stopped beneath a gas lamp, her face serious in the yellow light. "There's a woman named Anna Morrison who runs a boarding house for performers. She's been taking care of the musicians during the strike, making sure they don't starve while they fight this out." She paused. "As for work ... well, that depends on how this all ends."

"And how do you think it will end?"

Clara looked back toward the saloon where Cort's phonograph continued its mechanical performance. "I don't know. But I'll tell you one thing—I've never seen musicians more determined to fight for their lives. And I've never seen theater owners more scared of losing control."

She started to walk away, then turned back. "One more thing, Daniel. The musicians are meeting tomorrow night. Anna's boarding house, eight o'clock. If you're serious about finding work in this town, you'll want to be there."

As she disappeared into the shadows, Daniel stood alone beneath the gas lamp, his violin case heavy in his hand. Above him, the first stars were appearing over Elliott Bay, and somewhere in the distance, he could hear the sound of a real fiddle playing—not the mechanical reproduction of the phonograph, but the living, breathing voice of wood and strings and human heart.

He thought about Murphy's words in the saloon, about community and soul and the threads that held people together. Tomorrow night, he would go to Anna Morrison's boarding house. He would meet the other musicians. And he would discover what it meant to fight not just for work, but for the right of music to have a soul.

The wind picked up from the harbor, carrying with it the smell of salt and possibility. Daniel O'Malley pulled his coat tighter around him and walked toward his future, his grandfather's fiddle secure in his arms, ready to join the battle between human heart and mechanical progress.

In the distance, a church bell tolled nine o'clock, and the sound echoed off the hills like a call to arms.

2

THE MACHINE'S PROMISE

Seattle, Washington - February 1898

Daniel woke to the sound of hammering—not the rhythmic pounding of construction, but the sharp, desperate percussion of someone nailing boards over windows. Through the thin walls of Mrs. Patterson's rooming house, he could hear her muttering prayers in what sounded like Norwegian.

The morning light filtering through his single window revealed a city transformed overnight. Where yesterday there had been the chaotic energy of opportunity, today Daniel sensed something darker—the tightening grip of fear. He dressed quickly, strapping his violin case across his back, and made his way downstairs.

Mrs. Patterson stood in her parlor, hands on her hips, staring at a notice that had been slipped under her door.

She was a sturdy woman of perhaps fifty, with steel-gray hair and the calloused hands of someone who'd worked hard all her life.

"What's the trouble?" Daniel asked.

She looked up, her pale blue eyes reflecting worry. "You're the fiddle player from Chicago? The one Clara Weston brought around?"

"Yes, ma'am. Daniel O'Malley."

She thrust the paper at him. "Read this. My English isn't so good for the fancy words."

Daniel unfolded the notice. The letterhead read "Seattle Theater Owners Association" in elaborate script.

"Notice to All Musical Performers: Due to ongoing labor disputes and the availability of modern mechanical entertainment devices, the undersigned establishments will be conducting demonstrations of Edison Phonograph technology today at 2:00 PM at the Merchant's Hotel. All musicians currently seeking employment are encouraged to attend to witness the future of entertainment. Signed: John Cort, John W. Considine, Thomas Considine, Mose Goldsmith, H.L. Leavitt, Arthur G. Williams."

"Six names," Mrs. Patterson said grimly. "Six men who think they can replace God's gift of music with a machine."

Daniel folded the notice carefully. "They're trying to break the strike."

2 THE MACHINE'S PROMISE

"More than that," came a voice from the doorway. Clara Weston stepped into the parlor, her cheeks flushed from the cold morning air. "They're trying to break the spirit of every musician in the city."

She pulled off her gloves and warmed her hands by Mrs. Patterson's wood stove. "I've been to three boarding houses this morning. Every musician got the same notice. They want us all there, want us to see what we're up against."

"Are you going?" Daniel asked.

Clara's green eyes flashed. "Wouldn't miss it. But not for the reason they think." She lowered her voice. "Billy Murphy and the others are planning something. They want every musician who's still got fight left in them to show up."

Mrs. Patterson shook her head. "This will end in blood. Mark my words."

"Maybe," Clara said. "But it'll end one way or another. We can't go on like this—theaters closed, performers starving, the whole city's entertainment industry grinding to a halt."

Daniel thought about the scene he'd witnessed the night before in Cort's saloon. "What exactly are they planning?"

"I don't know," Clara admitted. "But I know Billy Murphy. He's not the type to give up without making his point."

By 1:30 that afternoon, a crowd had gathered outside the Merchant's Hotel on First Avenue. Daniel counted at least forty musicians in the throng—fiddlers, piano players, singers, even a man clutching a battered trumpet. They stood in small groups, their faces grim, their instruments cases clutched protectively against their chests.

The hotel itself was one of Seattle's finest, a four-story brick building that catered to the city's growing class of wealthy merchants and successful prospectors. Its lobby featured polished marble floors and crystal chandeliers, a stark contrast to the muddy streets and rough saloons that characterized most of the city.

"They picked their ground carefully," said a voice beside Daniel. He turned to find a tall, lean man with intelligent dark eyes and calloused fingers that marked him as a guitarist. "I'm James Scott," the man said, extending his hand. "Been traveling the railroad circuit between here and California. Heard about the trouble and came back to see what all the fuss was about."

"Daniel O'Malley. Just arrived from Chicago yesterday."

James whistled low. "Bad timing, friend. Or maybe good timing, depending on how you look at it." He nodded toward the hotel entrance, where well-dressed men were filing inside. "Those are the theater owners and their supporters. Business leaders, hotel owners, shipping magnates. They're all here to see the future."

Through the hotel's large windows, Daniel could see

chairs being arranged in the lobby. At the front of the room sat a table draped in white cloth, and on that table, gleaming like a shrine, was the largest phonograph Daniel had ever seen. It wasn't the modest home model he'd glimpsed in Cort's saloon the night before, but a massive commercial machine with a horn nearly three feet wide.

"Edison's latest," James said, following Daniel's gaze. "The Business Phonograph, they call it. Designed for public demonstrations and large spaces."

"You know about these machines?" James nodded grimly. "I've seen them in San Francisco and Sacramento. They're spreading up the coast like wildfire. Some places, they've already replaced live musicians entirely." He paused. "But I've also seen what happens to communities when the music dies. When there's no one left who can feel what a room needs, who can adapt to the moment."

A commotion near the hotel entrance drew their attention. Billy Murphy had arrived with a group of about fifteen musicians, including several Daniel recognized from the night before. Murphy himself carried a fiddle case, and his eyes swept the crowd with the calculating gaze of a general surveying a battlefield.

"Billy!" Clara called out, pushing through the crowd toward him. "What's the plan?"

Murphy's weather-beaten face creased into what might have been a smile. "The plan, darlin', is to give these gentlemen exactly what they want. A demonstration."

Before Clara could ask what he meant, the hotel doors

swung open and a man in an expensive suit stepped onto the front steps. Daniel recognized him from the previous evening—John Cort, one of the most powerful theater owners in the city.

"Gentlemen and ladies," Cort called out, his voice carrying easily across the crowd. "The demonstration will begin promptly at two o'clock. All are welcome to witness the future of entertainment."

The crowd began filing into the hotel lobby, musicians mixing uneasily with businessmen and curious onlookers. Daniel found himself swept along with James and Clara, the three of them ending up in chairs toward the back of the room.

The lobby buzzed with conversation as more people squeezed inside. Daniel estimated nearly a hundred people were now present, representing what seemed like every aspect of Seattle's entertainment and business communities. The air grew thick with the smell of wool coats, tobacco, and nervous perspiration.

At exactly two o'clock, John Cort stepped to the front of the room and raised his hand for silence.

"Ladies and gentlemen," he began, his voice carrying the practiced authority of a man accustomed to addressing crowds, "we gather today at a moment of great change in our city and our nation. Seattle has grown from a frontier town to a major commercial center in less than a decade, and our entertainment industry has grown with it."

He gestured toward the massive phonograph. "But

2 THE MACHINE'S PROMISE

growth requires adaptation. Progress demands that we embrace new technologies and new ways of doing business."

A murmur ran through the crowd of musicians, but Cort continued undeterred.

"For too long, the entertainment industry has been held hostage by the unreliable nature of human performers. Musicians who demand higher wages. Singers who refuse to perform certain songs. Orchestras that go on strike at the worst possible moments."

Daniel felt the tension in the room ratcheting higher. Several musicians shifted in their seats, hands clenching and unclenching.

"But today," Cort said, placing his hand on the phonograph with the reverence of a preacher touching a Bible, "I'm here to show you a better way. A more reliable way. The way of the future."

He cranked the handle on the side of the machine, and the large horn began to emit the opening notes of a popular waltz. But this wasn't the tinny reproduction Daniel had heard the night before—this machine filled the entire lobby with rich, full sound that seemed to come from everywhere at once.

The crowd leaned forward, impressed despite themselves. The recording was crisp and clear, the orchestra sounding almost as if it were present in the room. Daniel had to admit it was remarkable technology.

"No wages to pay," Cort said over the music. "No egos to manage. No strikes to endure. Simply perfect, consistent entertainment, available whenever and wherever you need it."

The waltz came to an end, and Cort replaced the cylinder with another. "Perhaps you'd prefer something more lively?" He started the mechanism again, and the room filled with the energetic rhythms of a military march.

Several of the businessmen began nodding approvingly. Daniel heard one man whisper to another, "Think of the savings. No musicians' salaries, no benefits, no—"

"No soul."

The voice cut through the recorded music like a knife. Billy Murphy had risen from his seat near the front of the room, his fiddle case in his hand.

Cort stopped the phonograph. "I beg your pardon?"

Murphy walked slowly toward the front of the room, his boots clicking on the marble floor. "I said it has no soul, Mr. Cort. Impressive machine, I'll grant you. Fine reproduction of sounds. But no soul."

"Soul is a luxury we can't afford in modern business," Cort replied coldly.

"Is it now?" Murphy began opening his fiddle case. "Tell me, can that machine of yours do this?"

He lifted his violin and bow, paused for a moment as

2 THE MACHINE'S PROMISE

if listening to something only he could hear, then began to play. But this wasn't the structured waltz or march that had come from the phonograph. This was something entirely different—a melody that seemed to capture the exact mood of the room, the tension and uncertainty and hope all woven together into something achingly beautiful.

As Murphy played, Daniel noticed something remarkable happening. The entire room seemed to breathe together. Businessmen who had been nodding approvingly at the phonograph now sat transfixed. Musicians who had been tense with anger now relaxed, their faces softening with recognition and pride.

The melody shifted, becoming more complex, incorporating fragments of Irish folk tunes, Norwegian hymns, and German drinking songs—all the musical traditions that the people in this room had brought with them from their homelands. It was as if Murphy was reading their hearts and playing their stories back to them.

Then, without missing a beat, he began to weave in the sounds of Seattle itself—the rhythm of hammers on construction sites, the call of ship horns from the harbor, the whistle of trains arriving with new dreamers and new dreams. The music became a living portrait of the city they all loved, the community they all shared.

When the last note faded, the silence in the room was profound.

Murphy lowered his violin and looked directly at Cort. "Can your machine do that, Mr. Cort? Can it feel what this room needs and give it exactly what it's hungry for?"

Cort's face had gone pale, but his voice remained steady. "That's very . moving, Billy. But businesses need reliability, not artistry."

"Do they now?" Murphy nodded toward the crowd. "Look around you, man. Look at their faces."

Daniel did look around, and what he saw surprised him. The businessmen weren't calculating costs anymore. They were remembering something—perhaps their own childhoods, their own dreams, their own reasons for coming to this wild city at the edge of the continent.

One of the men, a well-dressed gentleman Daniel didn't recognize, stood up. "Mr. Cort, I've heard your machine, and I'll admit it's impressive. But I've also heard Mr. Murphy play, and I'll tell you something— that man just reminded me why I fell in love with music in the first place."

Another man nodded. "My wife and I came to Seattle five years ago with nothing but hope and determination. We built our business from nothing, worked eighteen-hour days, sacrificed everything for success. But you know what kept us going? It was the music in the saloons and theaters. It was knowing that no matter how hard the work got, there would always be someone who could play our troubles away."

Cort held up a hand. "Gentlemen, please. Sentiment is all well and good, but—"

"It's not sentiment," interrupted a third man. Daniel recognized him as Mose Goldsmith, one of the theater owners whose name had been on the morning's notice. "It's good business. People don't just want entertainment, John. They want connection. They want to feel like they're part of something bigger than themselves."

Goldsmith rose from his seat and walked toward Murphy. "May I?" He gestured toward the violin.

Murphy hesitated, then handed over his instrument. Goldsmith examined it carefully, running his fingers along the strings and testing the tension of the bow.

"This violin," Goldsmith said to the crowd, "probably cost less than that phonograph. But look at what it can do." He handed the instrument back to Murphy. "It can adapt. It can respond. It can create something new every time it's played."

He turned to Cort. "John, I respect what you're trying to do. Modern technology, efficient business practices—these things have their place. But what if we're approaching this all wrong?"

"What do you mean?"

"What if the problem isn't the musicians? What if the problem is that we haven't been treating them like the valuable partners they are?"

A murmur ran through the crowd of musicians. Daniel saw Clara lean forward in her seat, her eyes bright with sudden hope.

Goldsmith continued. "These people—they're not just employees. They're artists. They're the ones who create the experiences that bring customers through our doors. What if instead of trying to replace them, we found a way to support them? To make sure they can make a decent living doing what they do best?"

"That's a fine sentiment," said Thomas Considine, another of the theater owners, "but business is business. We have responsibilities to our investors, our—"

He was interrupted by James Scott, who had risen from his seat in the back of the room. "Mr. Considine, if I may?" James walked forward, his guitar case in his hand. "I've been traveling between cities for the past two years, playing in theaters and saloons from San Francisco to Vancouver. And I'll tell you what I've observed."

He opened his case and lifted out a well-worn acoustic guitar. "The cities where musicians and theater owners work together—where there's mutual respect and fair compensation—those are the cities where the entertainment industry is thriving. The cities where owners try to squeeze every penny out of performers, or replace them with machines—those are the cities where the whole industry is dying."

James strummed a few chords, and Daniel was struck by the instrument's warm, rich tone. "In Sacramento, I played in a theater where the owner treated musicians as partners. We shared in the profits when shows were successful. We had input into programming. We were invested in the theater's success, and the theater was invested in ours."

He played a brief melody, something that sounded like a cross between a folk song and a hymn. "That theater is packed every night. Musicians from all over California want to play there. Audiences travel from other cities to see shows there. And the owner—he's making more money than any of his competitors."

James stopped playing and looked directly at the theater owners. "Gentlemen, you have a choice. You can try to replace human artistry with mechanical reproduction, and you might save some money in the short term. But in the long term, you'll lose the very thing that makes entertainment special—the connection between performer and audience, the magic that happens when human hearts communicate through music."

He strummed another chord, softer this time. "Or you can choose to work with us. You can choose to create something new—not just a business, but a community. A place where artists can thrive and audiences can experience something they can't get anywhere else."

The room fell silent again, but this silence felt different from before. Where there had been tension and confrontation, Daniel now sensed possibility.

Anna Morrison, who had been sitting quietly near the front of the room, stood up. She was a handsome woman of perhaps thirty-four, with dark hair and intelligent eyes that seemed to take in everything around her.

"If I may," she said, her voice carrying easily through

the room despite its gentle tone. "I've been housing and feeding many of these musicians during the strike. I've seen their struggles, their fears, their hopes. But I've also seen something else."

She looked around the room, making eye contact with both musicians and business owners. "I've seen them take care of each other. When one musician gets sick, the others pool their resources to pay for medicine. When someone's instrument gets damaged, they all chip in for repairs. When a performer's child needs shoes, the whole community makes sure that child doesn't go barefoot."

Her voice grew stronger, more passionate. "These people don't just make music together. They make community together. They look after each other. They understand that none of us succeeds unless all of us succeed."

She paused, letting her words sink in. "What if that's what Seattle needs? Not just better business practices, not just more efficient entertainment, but a real community? A place where people take care of each other, where everyone has a stake in everyone else's success?"

Daniel felt a chill run down his spine. There was something in Anna Morrison's voice, something prophetic, as if she were seeing a future that hadn't been born yet.

"What exactly are you suggesting, Mrs. Morrison?" asked H.L. Leavitt, another of the theater owners.

Anna smiled, and Daniel thought it was one of the most beautiful smiles he'd ever seen. "I'm suggesting that

2 THE MACHINE'S PROMISE

maybe this strike isn't a problem to be solved. Maybe it's an opportunity to create something entirely new. Something that's never existed before."

She looked at the musicians, then at the theater owners, then at the phonograph sitting silent on its white-draped table.

"What if we formed an organization—musicians and owners together—dedicated to taking care of each other? Not just during disputes, but all the time. Making sure everyone in the entertainment community has what they need to succeed. Creating a safety net so that no one falls through the cracks."

She paused, and when she spoke again, her voice carried the weight of deep conviction. "People helping people. That's what I'm talking about. Not charity from the top down, not business transactions, but genuine mutual aid. When one of us succeeds, we all succeed. When one of us struggles, we all help carry the load."

The room buzzed with quiet conversation as people turned to their neighbors, discussing Anna's proposal. Daniel saw businessmen nodding thoughtfully, musicians leaning forward with interest, and even John Cort looking less certain than he had at the beginning of the demonstration.

Billy Murphy raised his hand. "Mrs. Morrison, that sounds fine in theory. But what would it look like in practice?"

Anna's eyes lit up. "I don't know yet, Mr. Murphy. But

I know this—every great thing that's ever been built started with a simple idea: people helping people. Not because they have to, not because there's profit in it, but because that's what communities do."

She gestured toward the musicians, then toward the business owners. "Look around this room. We have people with different skills, different resources, different perspectives. But we all want the same thing—to see this city's music thrive, to see families fed, to see dreams fulfilled."

Her voice grew stronger. "What if we stopped thinking about 'us' and 'them'? What if we started thinking about just 'us'—one community, taking care of each other?"

She gestured toward the phonograph. "That machine can reproduce sounds. But it can't create community. It can't look after people. It can't build something larger than itself. It can't understand that the strongest foundation for any organization is people helping people."

She looked around the room one more time. "But we can."

As the crowd began to disperse, Daniel found himself walking slowly toward the hotel exit with James and Clara. The February afternoon was cold and gray, but something had changed. Where this morning there had been desperation and fear, now there was something that felt almost like hope.

"What do you think?" Clara asked quietly. "Can it

really work?"

James slung his guitar case over his shoulder. "I've seen stranger things happen. And I'll tell you one thing — Anna Morrison is right about community. In all my traveling, the places where musicians thrive are the places where everyone looks out for everyone else."

Daniel nodded, thinking about his grandfather's fiddle and the long journey that had brought him to this moment. "I came here looking for work," he said. "But maybe I found something more important."

"What's that?" Clara asked.

Daniel looked back at the hotel, where small groups of musicians and business owners were still talking on the front steps, their conversations animated and hopeful.

"A chance to be part of something bigger than just making music," he said. "A chance to help build a community."

As they walked back into the muddy streets of Seattle, Daniel could hear the sound of someone playing violin in the distance—not the mechanical reproduction of the phonograph, but the living, breathing voice of human artistry. It sounded like the beginning of something new.

Something that might change the world.

THE ORDER OF GOOD THINGS

3

THE BOARDING HOUSE

Seattle, Washington - February 1898

The boarding house at 412 Second Avenue looked unremarkable from the outside—a three-story wooden structure squeezed between a cobbler's shop and a Norwegian bakery. But as Daniel O'Malley approached in the gathering dusk, he could hear something that made his heart lift: the sound of music drifting from the windows. Not the mechanical reproduction of a phonograph, but the living, breathing harmony of human voices raised together in song.

Anna Morrison had given him the address after the demonstration at the Merchant's Hotel, along with a simple invitation: "Come see what 'people helping people' looks like."

Daniel paused on the front steps, listening. The song

was one he recognized from his childhood in Boston—an Irish ballad about finding home in a strange land. But the voices singing it carried accents from a dozen different countries, each adding their own flavor to the familiar melody.

He knocked softly on the door. "Come in, come in!" called a voice from inside. "We don't stand on ceremony here."

Daniel opened the door and stepped into a world that seemed to defy everything he'd been told about the hardships of the striking musicians. The front parlor was warm and bright, heated by a large wood stove and lit by several oil lamps. But what struck him most was the activity.

In one corner, a woman with Swedish features was mending a violin bow while a small child played with wooden blocks at her feet. Near the window, two men were carefully restringing a guitar, their conversation mixing English with what sounded like German. At a large table in the center of the room, several people were sorting through sheet music, and in the far corner, an elderly man was teaching a young woman how to tune a mandolin.

"Mr. O'Malley!" Anna Morrison emerged from what appeared to be the kitchen, wiping flour from her hands on her apron. "I'm so glad you decided to come."

She gestured around the bustling room. "As you can see, we keep busy here. Music may not be paying the bills right now, but that doesn't mean it stops."

3 THE BOARDING HOUSE

Daniel looked around in amazement. "How many people are staying here?"

"Eighteen musicians and their families at the moment," Anna replied matter-of-factly. "Some are regulars who live here permanently, others are just staying until the strike gets resolved. We make room for whoever needs it."

"But how do you manage it? The cost of feeding so many people..."

Anna smiled, and Daniel was struck again by the warmth and intelligence in her dark eyes. "Come with me. I'll show you."

She led him through the parlor toward the back of the house, stopping to make introductions as they went.

"This is Ingrid Larsen," she said, indicating the Swedish woman with the violin bow. "She's been teaching music to children in the Norwegian district. Ingrid, meet Daniel O'Malley—he's a fiddler from Chicago."

Ingrid looked up with a smile. "Chicago! I have a cousin in Chicago. Maybe you know him—Erik Larsen? He plays accordion?"

"I'm afraid not," Daniel said. "It's a big city."

"Not so big that musicians don't know each other," said one of the men working on the guitar. He stood and extended his hand. "Hans Mueller. I know at least six musicians in Chicago, and they all seem to know each other."

As they continued through the room, Anna pointed out more residents. "That's Giuseppe Torrino—he plays mandolin and teaches Italian songs. The young woman learning to tune is Sarah McKinnon; she's been singing in the Methodist church choir but wants to try her hand at theater work."

They paused by the sheet music table, where Daniel recognized Clara Weston sorting through a stack of compositions.

"Clara! I didn't expect to see you here."

She looked up with a grin. "Where else would I be? Anna's been feeding half the musicians in Seattle for the past month." She held up a piece of sheet music. "We're organizing all the arrangements and compositions that people have brought in. Some of these pieces have never been written down before— they've just been passed along from musician to musician."

"It's part of our library project," Anna explained. "We're collecting and preserving music that might otherwise be lost. Songs from the old countries, new compositions that musicians have written but never had the chance to publish."

She picked up a handwritten score. "This one is from Marcus McAllister—everyone calls him 'Dirty Laundry.' It's a song about working on the railroad that he learned from a crew chief in Montana. We're making copies so other musicians can learn it."

3 THE BOARDING HOUSE

Daniel examined the score, noting the complex interweaving of melody and rhythm. "This is remarkable work. But copying all of this by hand..."

"People helping people," said a familiar voice behind him. Daniel turned to find Marcus himself, a stocky man with prematurely gray hair and hands stained with what might have been coal dust or axle grease. "I write the songs down as best I can, Clara here fixes my spelling and makes the notes look proper, and Mrs. Morrison makes sure we have paper and ink."

Marcus gestured around the room. "Everyone contributes what they can. Some folks pay rent when they're working, others help with cooking or cleaning when they're not. Giuseppe there fixes instruments, Sarah helps teach the children their letters, Hans keeps our lamps burning bright."

"And when someone gets sick?" Daniel asked.

"We take care of them," Anna said simply. "Last week, one of our residents came down with pneumonia. Everyone pitched in to pay for medicine and to take turns sitting with him through the fever. That's what you do in a family."

She led Daniel toward the kitchen, where the source of the delicious smells he'd been noticing became apparent. Several women were working together to prepare what appeared to be dinner for a small army.

"Mrs. O'Brien manages our kitchen," Anna said, indicating a robust woman with Irish features who was stirring a large pot. "She used to cook for a logging camp up in Tacoma."

Mrs. O'Brien looked up with a smile. "And a fine thing it is, too, cooking for people who appreciate good food instead of just shoveling it down to get back to the trees." She ladled some of the stew into a bowl and handed it to Daniel. "Taste that and tell me if it's not better than what you'll get at any restaurant in town."

Daniel tasted the stew and had to admit it was excellent—rich with vegetables and herbs, with chunks of tender beef and potatoes. "This is wonderful. But how do you manage to feed so many people?"

"Same way we manage everything else," said Mrs. O'Brien. "People helping people. The Norwegian bakery next door gives us day-old bread. The butcher on Pike Street saves bones and scraps for our stew pot. The Italian grocer lets us have vegetables that are a little too ripe for his regular customers."

"And the musicians?" Anna added. "When they're working, they contribute to the food fund. When they're not working, they help with the shopping and preparation. Everyone gives what they can, everyone takes what they need."

They were interrupted by a commotion from the front parlor. Through the kitchen doorway, Daniel could see Billy Murphy entering with several other men, their faces grim and their voices raised in urgent conversation.

"Looks like the meeting's starting," Anna said. "Come

3 THE BOARDING HOUSE

on—this is what you really came to see."

Back in the parlor, Murphy was addressing the assembled musicians. "I've just come from meeting with some of the other theater owners," he announced. "Word of this afternoon's demonstration has spread, and there are mixed reactions."

"What kind of mixed reactions?" asked Clara.

"Well," Murphy said, settling into a chair by the fire, "Mose Goldsmith and H.L. Leavitt seem genuinely interested in Mrs. Morrison's idea about forming some kind of mutual aid organization. They've been talking about it all afternoon."

A murmur of hope ran through the room.

"But," Murphy continued, holding up a hand for silence, "John Cort and the Considine brothers are still convinced that phonographs are the answer to all their problems. They're talking about bringing in more machines, bigger ones, maybe even trying to record some of the local performers."

"Record us?" Sarah McKinnon looked alarmed. "You mean make those wax cylinder things with our voices on them?"

"That's exactly what I mean," Murphy said grimly. "Think about it—they record you once, pay you once, then use that recording forever. No more wages, no more negotiations, no more ." He gestured around the warm, bustling room. "No more community."

The room fell silent as the implications sank in. Daniel thought about the massive phonograph he'd seen that afternoon, imagining Clara's beautiful voice trapped forever in wax, unable to adapt or respond or create something new.

"So what do we do?" asked James Scott, who had arrived while they were in the kitchen.

Anna Morrison stood up slowly. She moved to the center of the room, where everyone could see her, and Daniel was struck by the natural authority she seemed to carry.

"We have a choice," she said quietly. "We can keep fighting the same fight—musicians against owners, tradition against progress, human against machine. Or we can try something different."

She looked around the room, making eye contact with as many people as possible. "This afternoon, I suggested that we form an organization based on the principle of people helping people. Some of you were there, some of you heard about it secondhand. But I want you all to understand what I mean."

She gestured around the boarding house. "Look at what we've built here, just in the past few weeks. We've created a place where musicians can survive during hard times. We've created a system where everyone contributes according to their ability and receives according to their need. We've created a family."

"That's all well and good," said Hans Mueller, "but

3 THE BOARDING HOUSE

Mrs. Morrison, this is just eighteen people. How do you expand something like this to include the whole city?"

Anna smiled. "The same way we started it here. One person at a time. One act of kindness at a time. One moment of choosing to help instead of hurt."

She moved to the window and looked out at the darkening street. "I've been thinking about this all afternoon, about what kind of organization could really make a difference. Not just for musicians, but for everyone who works for a living. Everyone who struggles to make ends meet. Everyone who dreams of something better."

She turned back to the room. "What if we created an organization that brought together people from all walks of life? Theater owners and performers, yes, but also shopkeepers and dock workers, teachers and seamstresses. All united around the idea that when we take care of each other, everyone prospers."

Billy Murphy leaned forward in his chair. "That sounds like what the labor unions are trying to do."

"Similar, but different," Anna replied. "Unions organize workers to fight owners. What I'm talking about is organizing everyone—workers and owners together—to fight the real problems: poverty, sickness, loneliness, despair."

She paused, gathering her thoughts. "Imagine if every member of this organization pledged to help any other member in need. Imagine if we created a network of mutual aid that stretched across the whole city, then across the territory, maybe even across the nation."

"You're talking about something that's never been done before," said Giuseppe Torrino.

"Exactly," Anna said, her eyes bright with passion. "Something new. Something that could change the world."

Daniel found himself caught up in her vision. "But how would it work? How would you organize something that large?"

Anna looked at him thoughtfully. "I think it would have to start small. Maybe with a group like the theater owners who met with us today—people who are already connected, who already have common interests. If we could get them to commit to the principle of people helping people, they could serve as the foundation."

James Scott spoke up from his corner. "The railroad musicians I know—we already help each other out informally. When someone's instrument breaks, we pool money for repairs. When someone gets sick, we make sure their family doesn't starve. What you're describing sounds like making that system official."

"And extending it beyond just musicians," added Clara. "Including everyone who makes the entertainment industry possible—the theater owners, the ticket sellers, the people who build and maintain the venues."

Anna nodded enthusiastically. "Yes! And then, once we've proven it works in one industry, we expand to others. Shopkeepers helping shopkeepers, dock workers helping

3 THE BOARDING HOUSE

dock workers, teachers helping teachers."

She paused, and when she spoke again, her voice carried a note of something almost prophetic. "I can see it in my mind—a great network of people committed to caring for each other. Not because government tells them to, not because employers require it, but because they choose to. Because they understand that none of us is truly successful until all of us have what we need to thrive."

Mrs. O'Brien, who had been listening from the kitchen doorway, spoke up. "That sounds like what my grandmother used to call 'the old way'—back in Ireland, before the landlords broke up the communities. Everyone looked after everyone else's children, everyone shared in the harvest, everyone mourned together and celebrated together."

"That's exactly right," Anna said. "The old way, but applied to the new world we're building here in America."

Marcus McAllister rubbed his chin thoughtfully. "It's a beautiful idea, Mrs. Morrison. But how do you get people to commit to something like that? How do you make sure they follow through?"

Anna was quiet for a moment, considering. Then she walked to a small bookshelf in the corner of the room and pulled out a well-worn Bible.

"My mother used to read to me from this," she said, opening to a passage she seemed to know by heart. "'Bear ye one another's burdens, and so fulfill the law of Christ.'" She looked up at the gathered musicians. "That's not just religious instruction. That's practical wisdom. When we carry each other's burdens, everyone's load gets lighter."

She closed the Bible and set it aside. "As for how we make sure people follow through—we don't force anyone. We just make it clear what the expectations are, and we trust that people will rise to meet them."

Billy Murphy stood up. "Mrs. Morrison, I've been thinking about what you said this afternoon, and what you're saying now. And I have to ask—are you talking about something that includes the theater owners? The same men who've been trying to break our strike?"

Anna nodded firmly. "Especially them. Billy, if we create an organization that excludes the people who disagree with us, what have we accomplished? We've just created another group to fight against, instead of working together."

She moved to stand directly in front of Murphy. "Think about Mose Goldsmith this afternoon. Think about how he looked when you played your fiddle. That man remembered why he fell in love with music in the first place. That's the person we need to reach—not the businessman worried about his profits, but the human being who understands the value of beauty and community."

Murphy was silent for a long moment. Then he nodded slowly. "You might be right. But it won't be easy."

"The best things never are," Anna replied. "But think about what we could accomplish. Think about a Seattle

3 THE BOARDING HOUSE

where no musician ever goes hungry, where no theater owner has to choose between profit and artistry, where everyone in the entertainment community looks out for everyone else."

She gestured toward the window again, where the lights of the city were beginning to twinkle in the darkness. "Think about families that never have to worry about medical bills because their community takes care of them. Think about children who grow up knowing that no matter what happens, there are people who will make sure they're safe and fed and loved."

The room fell silent again, but this time it was the silence of people imagining possibilities rather than contemplating problems.

James Scott broke the silence. "So what's the next step? How do we turn this vision into reality?"

Anna smiled, and Daniel thought it was the most hopeful expression he'd ever seen. "We start the way we always start. One person helping another person. And then we invite more people to join us."

She looked around the room. "Everyone here has already proven they believe in people helping people. You've been living it every day in this boarding house. Now we just need to extend that principle beyond these walls."

Clara raised her hand. "What about the theater owners? After this afternoon, some of them seemed genuinely interested. Should we approach them?"

"Yes," Anna said. "But carefully. We need to make it clear that we're not asking them to give up their businesses or their authority. We're asking them to join us in building something larger than any individual business—a community where everyone prospers."

Billy Murphy stood up again. "Mrs. Morrison, I'll be honest with you. A week ago, if someone had told me I'd be sitting in a room planning to work with John Cort instead of against him, I'd have said they were crazy."

He paused, looking around at the faces of his fellow musicians. "But seeing what you've built here, seeing how you've taken care of all of us during the worst times . maybe crazy is exactly what we need."

He extended his hand to Anna. "Count me in. Whatever this organization turns out to be, I want to be part of it."

One by one, the other musicians stood and added their agreement. Hans Mueller, Giuseppe Torrino, Sarah McKinnon, Marcus McAllister—each one pledging to help build this new kind of community.

When it came to Daniel's turn, he stood slowly, thinking about the long journey that had brought him to this moment. "I came to Seattle looking for work," he said. "But I think I found something more important. A chance to be part of something that could change the world."

As the evening wore on and the plans became more concrete, Daniel found himself thinking about Anna Morrison's vision of a network of mutual aid stretching

3 THE BOARDING HOUSE

across the nation. It seemed impossibly ambitious, but then again, so had the idea of feeding eighteen musicians in a boarding house, and here they were doing exactly that.

Just before midnight, as the meeting was breaking up, Anna pulled Daniel aside.

"I want you to know," she said quietly, "that what we're talking about tonight—this idea of people helping people—it's not just about musicians or theater owners or even Seattle. I believe this could be the foundation for something much larger."

"What do you mean?"

Anna looked toward the stairs, where several children were sleeping in rooms above. "I think about mothers, especially. The women who sacrifice everything to raise their children, who hold communities together, who provide the love and care that makes everything else possible. What if we created a culture where their contributions were truly valued? Where being a mother, being someone who nurtures and cares for others, was seen as the most important work in the world?"

Daniel was struck by the passion in her voice. "That sounds like something worth fighting for."

"Not fighting for," Anna corrected gently. "Building toward. Creating step by step, person by person, until it becomes the foundation of how we treat each other."

As Daniel walked back to his rooming house through the quiet streets of Seattle, he thought about the evening he'd just experienced. In the space of a few hours, he'd witnessed something remarkable—a group of people choosing hope over despair, cooperation over conflict, community over isolation.

Tomorrow, they would begin the work of turning Anna Morrison's vision into reality. They would approach the theater owners, not as adversaries, but as potential partners in building something entirely new.

And somewhere in the back of his mind, Daniel had the feeling that this was just the beginning—that what started in a boarding house on Second Avenue might one day spread far beyond the muddy streets of Seattle, carrying the simple but revolutionary principle of people helping people to communities across the nation.

The future, as John Cort had said, was arriving. But maybe it wouldn't be the mechanical, soulless future of phonographs and efficiency. Maybe it would be something warmer, more human—a future built on the understanding that the strongest foundation for any society was people choosing to take care of each other.

As he reached his own lodgings, Daniel could still hear the faint sound of music drifting from Anna's boarding house. Not a recording, not a mechanical reproduction, but the living voices of people who had chosen to create community together.

It sounded like the beginning of a revolution.

4

MORAN SHIPYARD

Seattle, Washington - February 6, 1898

The morning fog hung thick over Elliott Bay as Daniel O'Malley made his way toward the Moran Brothers' shipyard on South Charles Street. The February air was sharp with the smell of salt water and sawdust, and the sound of hammers echoed across the harbor as shipbuilders worked to meet the endless demand for vessels to carry gold-seekers north to Alaska.

It had been three days since the meeting at Anna Morrison's boarding house, three days of careful negotiations and tentative conversations between musicians and theater owners. Now, finally, both sides had agreed to meet on neutral ground—not in a fancy hotel where the owners held advantage, not in a musician's hall where the performers might feel more comfortable, but in the practical, working environment of Seattle's most successful shipyard.

Daniel clutched his violin case tighter as he approached the designated building. Through the morning mist, he could see other figures converging on the same spot—some he recognized as fellow musicians, others as the theater owners he'd observed at the phonograph demonstration. The very fact that they were all walking toward the same door felt like a small miracle.

"Nervous?"

Daniel turned to find James Scott falling into step beside him, guitar case slung across his back.

"Terrified," Daniel admitted. "What if it doesn't work? What if they can't find common ground?"

James smiled grimly. "Then we'll be no worse off than we were a week ago. But if it does work ." He gestured toward the shipyard, where the sounds of construction represented Seattle's booming economy. "If it does work, we might be part of building something as important as any of those ships."

They entered the building together, finding themselves in a large, open space that normally housed ship construction but had been cleared for the meeting. Wooden chairs were arranged in a rough circle, and several oil lamps provided warm light against the gray morning. The setting was deliberately informal— no head table, no podium, just a space where people could sit and talk as equals.

Anna Morrison was already present, arranging papers on a small side table. She looked up as Daniel and James entered, offering them an encouraging smile. "Good morning, gentlemen. Are you ready to make history?"

Before they could answer, the main door opened again and John Cort entered, followed by his fellow theater owners. Daniel recognized them from the phonograph demonstration: the Considine brothers, Mose Goldsmith, H.L. Leavitt, and Arthur Williams. They moved as a group, their expensive suits and confident bearing marking them clearly as the business community representatives.

For a moment, the two groups—musicians and owners—regarded each other across the open space. The tension was palpable, the weight of weeks of conflict and mistrust hanging heavy in the salt air.

Then Billy Murphy stepped forward, his fiddle case in hand, and extended it toward Mose Goldsmith.

"Mr. Goldsmith," he said quietly, "would you mind holding this while I shake your hand properly?"

Goldsmith looked surprised but took the offered instrument case. Murphy then extended his hand with a genuine smile. "Thank you for coming. I know this isn't easy for any of us."

The gesture seemed to break some invisible barrier. Goldsmith shook Murphy's hand, then carefully returned the fiddle case. "Thank you for the invitation, Billy. I'll admit, when Mrs. Morrison first approached me about this meeting, I wasn't sure what to expect."

"None of us were," said Anna, moving to the center

of the circle. "But that's exactly why we're here. To figure out together what we couldn't solve apart."

As people took their seats, Daniel found himself sitting between Clara Weston and Hans Mueller, directly across from Thomas Considine and H.L. Leavitt. The arrangement felt significant—not adversaries facing each other across battle lines, but community members gathering to solve a common problem.

Anna remained standing as the group settled. "Before we begin," she said, "I'd like to establish what we're trying to accomplish here. We're not here to re-litigate the strike or to assign blame for what's happened. We're here to see if we can build something new—something that serves everyone's interests."

John Cort cleared his throat. "Mrs. Morrison, I appreciate the sentiment, but let's be practical. We're businessmen with responsibilities to investors and customers. We can't make decisions based solely on good intentions."

"I wouldn't ask you to," Anna replied calmly. "Good business and good community can go hand in hand. In fact, I believe they must go hand in hand if either is going to thrive in the long term."

She moved to her side table and picked up a sheet of paper. "I've been doing some research since our last conversation. I'd like to share what I've learned about successful businesses in other cities— businesses that have found ways to treat their employees as partners rather than just hired help."

Daniel watched the theater owners' faces as Anna began to read examples from San Francisco, Portland, and even some eastern cities where cooperation between management and workers had led to increased profits, better employee retention, and stronger community relationships.

"The key principle," Anna concluded, "seems to be what I've been calling 'people helping people.' When businesses invest in their employees' well-being, those employees invest more of themselves in the business's success."

Arthur Williams leaned forward in his chair. "That's an interesting theory, Mrs. Morrison, but how does it work in practice? What would it look like in our industry?"

Billy Murphy spoke up. "If I may, Mr. Williams—I think it would look like musicians who feel valued and supported giving their best performances, night after night. It would look like performers who are invested in the success of the venues they work in, because they know that success benefits everyone."

"And from our perspective," added Mose Goldsmith, "it would look like reliable, dedicated performers who don't disappear when they get a better offer somewhere else. It would look like artists who actively help promote their venues because they see themselves as partners, not just employees."

Thomas Considine nodded thoughtfully. "But how

do we ensure that kind of mutual investment? How do we create a system that protects both sides' interests?"

Anna sat down in the circle, creating a more intimate atmosphere. "I believe we need to create an organization—something formal, with written principles and clear commitments. Something that brings together people from all aspects of the entertainment industry."

"Like a union?" asked H.L. Leavitt, and Daniel heard a note of wariness in his voice.

"Not exactly," Anna replied. "Unions are organized around the idea of workers versus owners. What I'm talking about is an organization built around the idea of everyone versus the problems that hurt us all— poverty, sickness, isolation, unfair competition."

James Scott set down his guitar case and leaned forward. "Mrs. Morrison, could you be more specific? What would this organization actually do?"

Anna's eyes lit up with the passion Daniel had seen at the boarding house. "It would provide mutual aid to any member in need. If a musician gets sick and can't work, the organization helps support their family. If a theater owner faces unfair competition or economic hardship, the organization rallies to help."

She paused, gathering her thoughts. "But more than that, it would create standards—for fair wages, for working conditions, for business practices. Standards that everyone agrees to uphold because everyone benefits from them."

John Cort had been silent through most of the discussion, but now he spoke up. "Mrs. Morrison, what you're describing sounds admirable, but how would such an organization be governed? Who would make decisions? How would disputes be resolved?"

"Together," Anna said simply. "Equal representation from all parts of the industry. Decisions made by consensus whenever possible, with clear procedures for handling disagreements."

Clara Weston raised her hand. "What about membership? Would it be limited to the entertainment industry, or could other people join?"

Anna smiled, and Daniel could see her vision expanding even as she spoke. "I think it should start with our industry—we know each other, we understand the challenges we all face. But eventually, I'd love to see it grow to include anyone who believes in the principle of people helping people."

She stood again, beginning to pace slowly around the circle. "Imagine if every merchant in Pike Place Market belonged to an organization dedicated to mutual aid. Imagine if dock workers and ship owners were united in supporting each other instead of fighting each other. Imagine if teachers and parents and city officials all worked together to make sure no child went hungry, no family went without shelter."

Her voice grew stronger, more passionate. "Imagine a Seattle where your success didn't depend on someone else's failure, where helping your neighbor was the smartest business strategy, where the whole community prospered together."

The room fell silent as people contemplated the scope of Anna's vision. Daniel found himself imagining what such a city would look like, what it would feel like to live in a place where mutual aid was the norm rather than the exception.

Billy Murphy broke the silence. "It's a beautiful dream, Mrs. Morrison. But how do we start? How do we turn a vision into reality?"

Anna returned to her seat. "We start small. We start here, in this room, with the people who are willing to try something new." She looked around the circle, making eye contact with each person. "We form an organization with a simple charter: to provide mutual aid and support to all members, to promote fair business practices, and to build stronger communities."

She pulled a sheet of paper from her stack. "I've drafted some initial principles, just to give us a starting point for discussion."

Daniel watched as she began to read:

"First: That all members commit to the principle of 'people helping people'—providing aid and support to fellow members in times of need, without expectation of direct repayment.

"Second: That all members agree to uphold fair

business practices—paying fair wages, providing safe working conditions, treating everyone with dignity and respect.

"Third: That all members participate in the democratic governance of the organization—sharing in decision-making, contributing to discussions, and helping to resolve disputes.

"Fourth: That all members work to expand the organization's reach and influence—inviting others to join, promoting the principles in their own communities, and working toward a society built on mutual aid and cooperation."

She looked up from the paper. "These are just suggestions. We can modify them, add to them, start over completely if needed. The important thing is that we all agree on the foundation we're building."

Mose Goldsmith raised his hand. "Mrs. Morrison, these principles are admirable, but I need to ask about practical matters. What would membership cost? How would the organization support itself financially?"

Anna nodded, clearly having anticipated this question. "I think membership should be based on ability to pay. Those who can afford more contribute more, those who can afford less contribute less. No one should be excluded because of financial hardship."

She gestured toward the theater owners. "Gentlemen, you have more resources than the musicians. But the musicians have something you need—their talent, their dedication, their connection to the community. Both sides bring value to the organization."

Arthur Williams spoke up. "What about leadership? Who would run this organization day-to-day?"

"We would," Anna replied. "All of us. I envision a council with representatives from different segments—theater owners, musicians, other community members as we grow. Decisions made collectively, leadership rotated regularly."

Thomas Considine leaned back in his chair, looking thoughtful. "Mrs. Morrison, I have to say, this is not what I expected when I agreed to this meeting. I thought we'd be negotiating an end to the strike, maybe discussing wage increases or working conditions."

He paused, seeming to choose his words carefully. "But what you're talking about is much more ambitious. You're talking about changing the entire relationship between business and labor."

"Yes," Anna said simply. "I am." "The question is," said H.L. Leavitt, "whether it's practical. Whether it can actually work in the real world of business and competition."

James Scott stood up slowly. "Mr. Leavitt, if I may share something I've observed in my travels." He looked around the circle. "I've played in cities where business owners and performers work together, and I've played in cities where they're constantly at war with each other."

He paused, gathering his thoughts. "The cities where they work together—those are the cities where the entertainment industry thrives. Audiences are larger, venues are more successful, musicians make better livings, and the whole community benefits from a vibrant cultural scene."

He gestured toward the window, where the sounds of Seattle's booming economy could be heard. "This city is growing fast, changing fast. You can either grow together or fight each other while the city grows around you."

Daniel felt compelled to speak. "I came to Seattle because I heard there were opportunities here for musicians. But in just a few days, I've learned something more important—I've learned what community can look like when people choose to help each other instead of competing."

He looked at the theater owners. "Gentlemen, you don't just need musicians who can play notes correctly. You need musicians who care about your venues' success, who will go the extra mile to make every performance special, who will help you build the kind of reputation that brings people back again and again."

He turned to his fellow musicians. "And we don't just need jobs. We need partners who understand the value of what we do, who will invest in our development as artists, who will help us build careers instead of just paying us for individual performances."

Clara Weston nodded enthusiastically. "Daniel's right.

What Mrs. Morrison is talking about isn't just good for individual businesses or individual musicians. It's good for the entire industry."

She stood up, her green eyes bright with conviction. "I've been thinking about this since the phonograph demonstration. Those machines can reproduce sounds, but they can't reproduce the relationship between performers and audiences. They can't create the sense of community that makes people want to come back to a venue again and again."

She gestured around the circle. "But if we can create an organization that strengthens those relationships, that makes everyone in the industry invested in everyone else's success, then we're not just competing with phonographs —we're offering something no machine can ever provide."

John Cort had been listening intently to the discussion. Now he spoke, his voice thoughtful rather than confrontational. "I'll be honest with all of you. When this strike began, I was convinced that the future lay with mechanical entertainment. Machines seemed more reliable, more predictable, more profitable."

He paused, looking around the circle. "But listening to this conversation, I'm beginning to understand something I hadn't considered before. Machines can reproduce performances, but they can't create the kind of loyalty and investment that comes from genuine partnership."

He looked directly at Billy Murphy. "Billy, when you

played at the demonstration the other day, you didn't just play music. You created a moment that brought the entire room together. That's not something that can be mechanically reproduced."

Murphy nodded. "That's what music is supposed to do, Mr. Cort. It's supposed to create connection, build community, bring people together."

"Then maybe," Cort said slowly, "what we should be doing is figuring out how to support that kind of connection, rather than trying to replace it."

Anna Morrison had been quiet during this exchange, but now she leaned forward with excitement. "Mr. Cort, are you saying you'd be interested in joining this organization we're discussing?"

Cort looked around at his fellow theater owners, then at the musicians, then back at Anna. "Mrs. Morrison, I'm saying I think you might be onto something. Something that could benefit all of us."

He stood up, beginning to pace as Anna had done earlier. "What if we created an organization that was actually a competitive advantage? What if being a member meant you were part of a network of the best musicians, the most ethical theater owners, the most community-minded businesses in the city?"

The energy in the room was shifting, Daniel realized. Where there had been tentative exploration, now there was genuine excitement.

Mose Goldsmith stood as well. "Mrs. Morrison, I'd like to propose something. What if we don't just talk about this organization—what if we actually form it? Here, today, in this room."

The suggestion sent a shock of possibility through the group. Daniel felt his heart racing as he contemplated what Goldsmith was proposing.

Anna looked around the circle. "Are you serious, Mr. Goldsmith? Are you all willing to take that step?"

One by one, the people in the circle began to nod. Theater owners and musicians, business leaders and artists, all united around the vision of something new and unprecedented.

Billy Murphy stood up. "Mrs. Morrison, if we're going to do this, we need to do it right. We need a name, we need formal principles, we need structure."

Anna smiled, and Daniel thought it was the most radiant expression he'd ever seen. "I've actually been thinking about a name," she said. "What about . the Order of Good Things?"

The name hung in the salt air of the shipyard, and Daniel felt something click into place. The Order of Good Things. It captured everything they'd been talking about—the commitment to goodness, to community, to building something positive instead of just fighting against what was wrong.

"I like it," said James Scott. "It suggests both

organization and aspiration."

Clara Weston nodded enthusiastically. "It sounds like something worth belonging to."

Thomas Considine raised his hand. "Before we get too carried away, we need to discuss practical matters. How will this organization be structured? What will the membership requirements be? How will we handle finances?"

"And," added H.L. Leavitt, "we need to be clear about what we're committing to. If I join this organization, what exactly am I promising to do?"

Anna moved back to her side table and picked up another sheet of paper. "I've given some thought to that as well. May I suggest a simple pledge that all members would make?"

She cleared her throat and began to read:

"I pledge to support my fellow members in times of need, to conduct my business with honesty and fairness, to treat all people with dignity and respect, and to work toward a community where people help people."

The simplicity of the pledge was striking. No complex legal language, no detailed requirements, just four basic commitments that captured the essence of what they'd been discussing.

Arthur Williams nodded approvingly. "Short enough to remember, comprehensive enough to mean something."

Billy Murphy walked to the center of the circle. "Mrs. Morrison, with your permission, I'd like to be the first person to take that pledge."

Anna looked around the circle. "If others are willing to join him, I think we can consider the Order of Good Things officially founded."

One by one, the people in the circle stood and spoke the pledge aloud. Theater owners and musicians, business leaders and artists, all committing to the same principles of mutual aid and community support.

When it was Daniel's turn, he felt the weight of history in the words. "I pledge to support my fellow members in times of need, to conduct my business with honesty and fairness, to treat all people with dignity and respect, and to work toward a community where people help people."

As the last person finished speaking, Anna looked around the circle with tears in her eyes. "Ladies and gentlemen, I think we've just witnessed the birth of something remarkable."

She moved to the center of the circle. "The Order of Good Things is now officially founded. We are the charter members, and our first task is to prove that this vision can work."

John Cort stepped forward. "Mrs. Morrison, before we adjourn, I think we need to address the immediate situation. The strike is still ongoing, theaters are still closed, and people are still out of work."

Anna nodded. "You're absolutely right, Mr. Cort. Our first act as an organization should be to resolve the conflict that brought us together."

She looked at the theater owners. "Gentlemen, are you willing to reopen your theaters and rehire the musicians at fair wages?"

"More than that," said Mose Goldsmith. "I'm willing to offer the musicians a share in the profits when shows are successful. True partnership, as we've been discussing."

The other theater owners quickly agreed, and within minutes they had worked out terms that would end the strike and establish the Order of Good Things as a functioning organization.

As the meeting broke up and people began to gather their belongings, Daniel found himself standing beside Anna Morrison.

"Mrs. Morrison," he said quietly, "do you really think this will work? Can something started in one shipyard meeting really change the world?"

Anna looked out the window at the busy harbor, where ships were being built to carry dreams north to Alaska. "Daniel, every great journey starts with a single step. Every mighty river starts with a single spring. Every community starts with a few people deciding to take care of each other."

She turned back to him with a smile. "We've taken the first step today. Now we have to see how far this river will flow."

As Daniel walked back through the streets of Seattle that afternoon, he could already see changes beginning. The "Closed Due to Labor Dispute" signs were coming down from theater windows. Musicians were emerging from boarding houses with their instruments, ready to return to work. Business owners were shaking hands with performers, discussing not just immediate employment but long-term partnerships.

But more than that, he could sense something in the air—a feeling of possibility, of community, of people choosing to build something together rather than tear each other apart.

The Order of Good Things had been born. And Daniel had the feeling that Anna Morrison was right—this was just the beginning of something that could change the world.

That evening, as music once again filled the theaters and saloons of Seattle, the sound carried with it a new harmony—the harmony of people who had chosen to help each other, to build community, to create an order of good things that could last for generations.

The future had arrived, just as John Cort had predicted. But it wasn't the mechanical future of phonographs and efficiency. It was something warmer, more human—a future built on the revolutionary principle that the strongest foundation for any society was people choosing to take care of each other.

And in a boarding house on Second Avenue, Anna Morrison sat by her window, listening to the music and dreaming of the day when this same spirit of mutual aid and community support might spread to every corner of the nation, creating a culture where mothers and fathers, workers and owners, neighbors and strangers all understood that their greatest strength lay in helping each other thrive.

"I can almost see it," Anna said, her eyes distant. "Some other woman, maybe even another Anna—" she laughed at the thought "—championing mothers across the whole nation."

THE ORDER OF GOOD THINGS

5

JOURNEY SOUTH

En Route to Sacramento, California - March 1899

The Southern Pacific locomotive pulled away from Seattle's King Street Station with a long, mournful whistle that seemed to echo Daniel O'Malley's mixed feelings about leaving the city that had become home. Through the rain-streaked window of the passenger car, he watched the muddy streets and hastily-built structures of Pioneer Square disappear into the distance, replaced by the evergreen forests and rolling hills of western Washington.

"Having second thoughts?" Clara Weston asked softly, settling into the seat beside him. She wore a traveling dress of deep blue wool, practical but elegant, and her auburn hair was pinned up beneath a small hat that matched her outfit perfectly.

Daniel turned from the window to look at her, still amazed that she had agreed to come with him on this journey. "Not about the mission," he said. "The Fraternal Order of Eagles needs to expand, and Sacramento seems like the logical place to start. But leaving Seattle..." He gestured toward the window.

"A year ago, I never would have imagined I'd think of any place as home."

Clara smiled, and Daniel felt his heart skip slightly. Their relationship had grown slowly over the months since the F.O.E.'s founding, built on shared work and common purpose. But somewhere along the way, what had begun as partnership had deepened into something more precious.

"Home isn't a place," she said, placing her gloved hand over his. "It's the people you choose to build a life with."

Before Daniel could respond to the implications of her words, James Scott appeared in the aisle beside their seats, his guitar case slung across his back and a grin on his weathered face.

"Mind if I join you two lovebirds?" he asked, settling into the seat across from them without waiting for an answer. "I've been looking forward to showing you California. It's a different world from Seattle—older, more established, and full of wonders you've never seen."

Daniel felt his cheeks redden at James's casual reference to him and Clara as "lovebirds," but Clara seemed unperturbed. "What kind of wonders?" she asked.

James leaned forward conspiratorially. "Well, for starters, Sacramento has electric streetlights. Not gas lamps

5 JOURNEY SOUTH

like Seattle, but actual electric lights powered by that new powerhouse they built up in Folsom. The whole city glows at night like something out of a fairy tale."

"Electric lights?" Daniel had heard rumors of such things but had never seen them himself. "How is that possible?"

"They've got this massive powerhouse twenty-two miles away in Folsom," James explained, his eyes bright with enthusiasm. "Biggest in the world, they say. It harnesses the power of the American River and sends electricity all the way to Sacramento through wires strung on poles. The whole thing went into operation about four years ago."

Clara leaned forward, intrigued. "But how does electricity travel that far without losing power?"

"That's the miracle of it," James said. "They figured out how to send it at very high voltage—something like 11,000 volts—then step it down when it reaches the city. It's like... like having one enormous power source that can light up an entire community."

Daniel was struck by something in James's description. "That sounds almost like what happened with our own organization—one source of strength supporting many communities."

"Exactly!" James said, pointing at Daniel. "Remember how quickly things grew once word spread about the Order of Good Things? We went from Anna Morrison's boarding house meetings to over two hundred members in just six months."

Clara nodded thoughtfully. "And when we chose the eagle as our symbol—that was when everything really came together. Something about that image of soaring above petty disputes, watching out for the whole community."

"The Brotherhood," Daniel added, feeling a surge of pride at the memory. "When we made the name change to the Fraternal Order of Eagles official, it felt like we were finally becoming what Anna had always envisioned."

James settled back in his seat with a satisfied expression. "And now you're carrying that vision to California. Wait until you see what else they've got in Sacramento. There are people driving around in electric carriages—no horses, just batteries and motors. Silent as ghosts and clean as a whistle."

"Electric carriages?" Clara's eyes widened. "You mean automobiles?"

"That's right. Though they've got steam cars too, and some experimental gasoline ones. It's like the whole future is being invented at once." James leaned forward again. "But the electric ones are something special. Perfect for city driving—quiet, no smoke, no manure to clean up."

As the train wound its way south through the Cascade Mountains, James regaled them with stories of the changing world they were entering. He spoke of theaters in Sacramento that were lit entirely by electricity, making performances possible at any hour. He described restaurants with electric fans that kept diners cool even in

5 JOURNEY SOUTH

the heat of California summers. He painted pictures of a city where technology served people rather than replacing them.

"The key," he said, "is that Sacramento has figured out how to use these new inventions to enhance what people do, not eliminate the need for people to do it."

Daniel thought about the phonographs that had threatened to replace musicians in Seattle. "You mean they've found a balance?"

"More than that," James replied. "They've found a way to make technology serve community instead of destroying it. Electric lights make theaters safer and more comfortable, so more people come to hear live music. Electric streetcars make it easier for audiences to get to performances. Even those electric automobiles—they're bringing people together rather than isolating them."

As they talked, the train began its descent from the mountains into the Central Valley of California. The landscape outside changed dramatically—from the dense forests of the Pacific Northwest to golden grasslands dotted with oak trees. The air grew warmer, and Daniel could smell something different through the open windows: the scent of a land that seemed to promise abundance.

"Tell me about the music scene in Sacramento," Clara said. "What should we expect when we start talking to people about the Fraternal Order of Eagles?"

James considered the question carefully.

"Sacramento's different from Seattle," he said finally. "Seattle is still a frontier boomtown—rough around the edges, everyone scrambling to make their fortune. Sacramento's the state capital, more established, more... refined, I suppose."

He pulled out a small notebook and flipped through several pages. "The entertainment district is centered around K Street and the riverfront. There are maybe a dozen serious theaters and music halls, plus countless saloons and smaller venues. The performers tend to be more professional, the audiences more sophisticated."

"More competition for us?" Daniel asked.

"Different competition," James replied. "In Seattle, you were competing with phonographs and economic desperation. In Sacramento, you'll be competing with tradition and established ways of doing business."

Clara frowned. "What do you mean?"

"Well," James said, "Sacramento's entertainment industry has been running the same way for twenty years. Theater owners and musicians have established relationships, established practices. They might not see the need for something like the Fraternal Order of Eagles."

Daniel felt a flutter of concern. "So they might not be interested in what we're offering?"

James smiled reassuringly. "Oh, they'll be interested. The question is whether they'll be willing to change. But that's where you two come in." He gestured between Daniel

5 JOURNEY SOUTH

and Clara. "You've got something they don't have—proof that a different way is possible."

"What do you mean?" Clara asked.

"Look at yourselves," James said. "A year ago, you were struggling musicians in a city torn apart by labor disputes. Now you're partners in a thriving organization with the eagle as your guide, traveling as ambassadors for a Brotherhood that's changing how people think about business and community. "He leaned forward earnestly. "You're not just carrying a message about the Fraternal Order of Eagles.

You're living proof that it works. You've seen how quickly the membership grew when people understood what we were offering—not just better wages or working conditions, but genuine fraternal bonds."

As the afternoon wore on and the train approached the Sacramento Valley, Daniel found himself thinking about James's words. Was he really so different from the person who had stepped off the train in Seattle just over a year ago? That Daniel had been focused solely on his own survival, his own success. This Daniel was traveling hundreds of miles to help build something larger than himself—something that now bore the proud name of the Fraternal Order of Eagles and had grown beyond anything Anna Morrison had initially imagined.

And Clara—the change in her was even more remarkable. The ambitious young woman who had been torn between personal success and solidarity with her fellow musicians had become a confident leader, someone who could articulate the vision of the Brotherhood as clearly as Anna Morrison herself.

"Penny for your thoughts," Clara said softly. The afternoon sun streaming through the window caught the red highlights in her hair, and Daniel was struck by how beautiful she looked.

"I was thinking about change," he said. "About how much we've both changed since that first night at Anna's boarding house. And about how far the organization has come—from the Order of Good Things to the Fraternal Order of Eagles, from a handful of people to a real Brotherhood."

Clara nodded thoughtfully. "Do you ever wonder what would have happened if we hadn't met? If the strike had been resolved some other way, if the F.O.E. had never been formed?"

Daniel considered the question. "I think I would have spent my life playing music in saloons and small theaters, earning just enough to get by, never really connecting with anyone or anything larger than my next meal."

"And I think I would have eventually made it to San Francisco or maybe even New York," Clara said. "I would have had some success, maybe even become famous. But I don't think I would have been happy."

"Why not?"

Clara was quiet for a moment, looking out at the

passing landscape. "Because success without purpose is just... hollow. What we're doing now, building the Brotherhood, creating community—that feels like it matters."

Daniel felt his heart swell with affection for her. "Clara, I need to tell you something." She turned to face him fully, her green eyes serious. "What is it?"

"I..." Daniel hesitated, suddenly aware that James was sitting just across from them, though the older man seemed to be dozing. "I love you."

The words hung in the air between them, and for a moment Daniel was terrified that he had made a mistake, that he had misread the growing intimacy between them.

Then Clara smiled, and it was like sunshine breaking through clouds. "I love you too, Daniel. I think I have for months, but I wasn't sure if..."

"If what?"

"If it was possible to build a romantic relationship and a working partnership at the same time. If we could be lovers and still be effective as organizers for the Fraternal Order of Eagles."

Daniel reached for her hand, no longer caring if James or anyone else might see them. "I think," he said, "that love and shared purpose might actually make us stronger at both."

Clara squeezed his hand. "Anna Morrison would say

it's another example of people helping people—just like the Brotherhood itself."

They were interrupted by James stirring in his seat across from them. He opened his eyes, looked at their joined hands, and grinned. "Well, it's about time you two figured that out. I was beginning to wonder if I'd have to lock you in a closet together."

Daniel and Clara both laughed, and the tension of the moment dissolved into something warm and comfortable.

"Just remember," James added with mock seriousness, "you're representing the Fraternal Order of Eagles now. Try to be good examples of what love and partnership can look like within the Brotherhood."

As evening approached, the train began to slow for its approach to Sacramento. Through the windows, Daniel could see the first evidence of the wonders James had described. Electric lights were beginning to come on throughout the city, creating pools of bright, steady illumination that were completely different from the flickering gas lamps of Seattle.

"My God," Clara breathed, pressing her face to the window. "It's like daylight."

Indeed, the electric streetlights cast a clear, white glow that made the city visible in remarkable detail. Daniel could see people walking along sidewalks, carriages moving through streets, and in the distance, what appeared to be vehicles moving without any horses pulling them.

5 JOURNEY SOUTH

"Are those the electric automobiles?" he asked James.

James looked out the window and nodded. "Some of them. You can tell because they move so smoothly and quietly. The steam cars make more noise, and the gasoline ones—well, you can smell those from a mile away."

As they pulled into Sacramento's Central Pacific Railroad station, Daniel was struck by the scale and sophistication of the facility. It was easily twice the size of Seattle's station, with electric lights illuminating the platform and what appeared to be electric fans keeping the air circulating in the waiting areas.

"Welcome to the future," James said as they gathered their belongings and prepared to disembark. Daniel picked up his violin case with one hand and helped Clara with her traveling bag with the other. As they stepped onto the platform, he was immediately struck by the different atmosphere of Sacramento.

Where Seattle had felt raw and urgent, Sacramento felt established and confident. The people moved more slowly, dressed more formally, and seemed less driven by the desperate energy of a frontier boomtown.

"It's beautiful," Clara said, looking around at the electric-lit station. "But it's also a bit intimidating."

"That's exactly how I felt the first time I came here," James said. "But remember, underneath all this sophistication, these are still people who love music, who want to be entertained, who face the same basic challenges as everyone else."

They made their way through the station toward the street, where James had promised to show them some of the city's marvels before they settled in for the night. As they stepped outside, Daniel was struck by the clarity of the electric streetlights and the relative quiet of the city—punctuated occasionally by the ring of a telephone bell from a nearby hotel and the gentle whir of bicycles passing by.

"Look at that," Clara said, pointing to a young man pedaling past on a gleaming bicycle, a violin case strapped to his back. "Even the musicians here have found ways to adapt to the new technology."

Then they heard it—the soft, almost silent approach of an electric automobile. The vehicle glided up to the station entrance like something from a dream. It was shaped like a traditional carriage but with no horses, no steam, no visible means of propulsion. A well-dressed man sat behind what appeared to be a steering mechanism, and beside him sat a woman in an elegant evening dress.

"Good evening," the man called out as he brought the vehicle to a stop. "Are you folks looking for transportation? I run a taxi service with the latest electric automobiles."

Daniel stared in amazement. The vehicle was beautiful—polished wood and brass, with comfortable-looking seats upholstered in fine leather. But what struck him most was how quiet it was. No clattering of hooves, no hissing of steam, just a barely audible hum that seemed to come from somewhere beneath the passenger compartment.

5 JOURNEY SOUTH

"How fast does it go?" Clara asked, her curiosity overcoming any nervousness.

"Twelve miles per hour on level ground," the driver replied proudly. "And it can run for forty miles on a single charge of the batteries. Perfect for city driving."

James stepped forward. "We're looking for lodging near the theater district. Do you know the area?"

"Know it?" The driver grinned. "I live in it. I'm Marcus Reynolds, and I play piano at the Golden Eagle Theater when I'm not driving this contraption. Hop in, and I'll give you the grand tour." As they climbed into the electric automobile, Daniel felt as if he were entering another world. The seats were comfortable, the ride was remarkably smooth, and the quiet operation allowed for easy conversation.

"You're a musician?" Clara asked Marcus as they glided through the electric-lit streets.

"Piano, some violin, a little singing when they need it," Marcus replied. "Been playing in Sacramento for fifteen years now. It's a good living if you know how to work with the theater owners."

Daniel and Clara exchanged glances. This was exactly the kind of person they needed to talk to about the Fraternal Order of Eagles.

"We're from Seattle," Daniel said carefully. "We've been involved in organizing musicians up there, trying to create better working relationships with theater owners."

Marcus glanced back at them with interest. "Oh? What kind of organizing?"

"It started as something called the Order of Good Things," Clara said. "But it grew so quickly—over two hundred members in just six months—that we chose the eagle as our symbol and officially became the Fraternal Order of Eagles. It's a Brotherhood that brings together musicians and theater owners as partners rather than adversaries."

"Partners?" Marcus sounded intrigued. "And you said it's a Brotherhood? Tell me more."

As they drove through Sacramento's electric-lit streets, James began to explain the principles of the F.O.E. while Daniel and Clara added details about their experiences in Seattle—how rapidly the membership had grown once word spread, how the eagle symbol had unified everyone around a shared vision of soaring above petty disputes, how the formal establishment of the Brotherhood had created lasting bonds between members.

Marcus listened intently, asking thoughtful questions and occasionally pointing out landmarks as they passed.

"That's remarkable," he said as they turned onto K Street, the heart of Sacramento's entertainment district. "We've been talking for years about needing something like that here. The relationship between musicians and theater owners has been... well, let's call it cordial but not particularly warm."

He brought the electric automobile to a stop in front

5 JOURNEY SOUTH

of a three-story building with "The Golden Eagle Theater" painted in elegant script above the entrance. Electric lights illuminated the facade, and Daniel could see people in evening dress entering for what appeared to be a late performance.

"This is my main venue," Marcus said. "Good owner, treats musicians fairly, but there's always room for improvement." He turned to face them. "Would you be interested in meeting some of the local performers? I could arrange a gathering tomorrow evening."

Daniel felt his heart race with excitement. Their first day in Sacramento, and they already had a potential contact and the possibility of a meeting.

"We'd be very interested," Clara said. "Though I should warn you, what we're talking about isn't just better working conditions for musicians. It's about creating a whole new kind of community—a true Brotherhood."

Marcus smiled. "Miss, after fifteen years in this business, I'm ready to try anything that might make it better. Besides," he gestured around at the electric lights and smooth streets, "Sacramento's a city that believes in progress. Maybe it's time we applied some of that progressive thinking to how we treat each other."

As Marcus helped them unload their luggage at a nearby hotel, Daniel felt a sense of possibility that reminded him of that first meeting in Anna Morrison's boarding house—and of the excitement that had built as the membership grew and the eagle symbol was chosen. People wanted to belong to something larger than themselves. They wanted their work to have meaning and their lives to have purpose. They wanted to know that if they fell, someone would be there to help them up. The rapid growth of the F.O.E. in Seattle had proved that.

"Tomorrow evening, then," Marcus said as he prepared to drive away in his silent electric automobile. "Seven o'clock at the Golden Eagle. I'll invite some of the other musicians and maybe a theater owner or two."

As the electric automobile glided away into the night, Daniel and Clara stood on the sidewalk holding hands and looking up at the electric streetlights of Sacramento.

"What do you think?" Clara asked. "Can the Fraternal Order of Eagles work here?"

Daniel squeezed her hand and thought about everything they had experienced since leaving Seattle that morning—the journey through changing landscapes, the declaration of their love for each other, the encounter with Marcus Reynolds and his electric automobile. He thought too of how far they'd come from Anna Morrison's simple idea, through the rapid expansion that had led them to adopt the eagle as their symbol and formally establish the Brotherhood.

"I think," he said, "that we're about to find out that the eagle's vision works anywhere people are willing to soar together."

Above them, the electric lights powered by the distant Folsom Powerhouse cast their steady glow over a city that had learned to harness the power of technology in service of human community. And somewhere in the distance, Daniel could hear the sound of music drifting from the theaters and saloons—not mechanical reproduction, but the living, breathing voices of human performers creating connection and joy.

The Fraternal Order of Eagles had come to California. And Daniel had the feeling that this was just the beginning of something that could transform not just the entertainment industry, but the entire way Americans thought about work, community, and caring for each other. As they walked into their hotel, hand in hand, he whispered to Clara, "We're going to change the world."

"Together," she whispered back. "The Brotherhood helping people, one city at a time."

Outside, the electric lights of Sacramento continued their steady glow, powered by the revolutionary technology that proved what Anna Morrison had always known—that when individual sources of strength came together to serve a common purpose, like eagles soaring in formation, they could illuminate an entire community.

THE ORDER OF GOOD THINGS

6

THE GOLDEN EAGLE

Sacramento, California - March 1899

The Golden Eagle Theater at seven o'clock in the evening was a testament to the power of electricity. Every corner of the ornate interior was illuminated by Edison bulbs that cast a warm, steady glow over red velvet seats and gold-painted balconies. Daniel O'Malley stood in the wings, watching stagehands move scenery with an efficiency that would have been impossible under gas lighting, and marveled at how technology could enhance rather than replace human artistry.

"Impressive, isn't it?" Marcus Reynolds appeared beside him, carrying a well-worn guitar case. "When they first installed electric lighting three years ago, it changed everything. Performances could run later, rehearsals could be more precise, and the fire risk..." He shook his head. "Well, let's just say we all sleep better at night."

Daniel nodded, thinking about the gas-lit theaters of Seattle with their constant danger of flames and their limited evening schedules. "It's remarkable what's possible when technology serves people instead of replacing them."

"Speaking of which," Marcus said, "the folks are gathering backstage. Are you ready to talk about this Fraternal Order of Eagles?"

They made their way through the wings to a large rehearsal room behind the main stage. Daniel was struck immediately by the diversity of the group Marcus had assembled. There were perhaps twenty people present—musicians ranging from a young woman with a mandolin to an elderly man with a bass violin, plus several individuals Daniel recognized as theater owners or managers from their fine clothing and confident bearing.

Clara was already there, deep in conversation with a group of female performers. James Scott sat in a corner tuning his guitar while talking with two other string players. The atmosphere was relaxed but expectant, like the moments before a performance when everyone knows something important is about to happen.

"Everyone, everyone!" Marcus called out, gesturing for attention. "Thank you all for coming tonight. I'd like to introduce our guests from Seattle—Daniel O'Malley, Clara Weston, and James Scott. They've got some interesting ideas about how musicians and theater owners can work together."

As Daniel stepped forward to address the group, he

noticed one of the guitar players examining James Scott's instrument with obvious interest.

"Excuse me," the man said, "but is that a Martin?"

James looked up from his tuning. "It is indeed. Style 28, rosewood back and sides, built in Nazareth about five years ago. You know Martins?"

"I should hope so," the man replied with a grin. "I'm Thomas Wright, and I've been playing guitars for fifteen years. That's a beautiful instrument—you can hear the quality in every note."

Another guitarist, a younger man with callused fingers, leaned forward. "I've got a Washburn myself," he said, patting his case. "Chicago-made, 1896. Not as fancy as a Martin, but it's served me well through two years of theater work."

"May I see it?" James asked with genuine interest.

As the young man—who introduced himself as Paul Martinez—opened his case, a small crowd gathered around the instruments. Daniel realized this was exactly the kind of moment that made live music irreplaceable—musicians sharing their knowledge and passion with each other.

"The Washburn's got a different voice than the Martin," James observed as Paul handed over his guitar. "Brighter, more direct. Perfect for theater work where you need to cut through other instruments."

He strummed a few chords, nodding approvingly.

"George Washburn knew what he was doing when he started making instruments for working musicians. This has got excellent intonation and a strong, clear tone."

Thomas Wright pulled out his own instrument, a guitar Daniel didn't recognize. "This is something a bit different," Thomas said. "It's made by a fellow named Orville Gibson up in Kalamazoo, Michigan. He's been experimenting with arched tops instead of flat ones, like violin makers use."

Daniel leaned in to examine the Gibson guitar. It was indeed different from both the Martin and the Washburn —the top was carved and arched rather than flat, and the overall construction seemed more robust.

"Gibson's only been making guitars for a couple of years," Thomas continued, "but his approach is revolutionary. He carves the top and back from solid wood, which gives more volume and projection."

James took the Gibson and played a few notes, his eyebrows rising in surprise. "That's remarkable. It's got the power of a Martin but with more focus, more punch. How does it sound in a theater setting?"

"That's what makes it special," Thomas replied. "When I'm playing in the orchestra pit, this guitar can hold its own against brass and woodwinds. The arched top design just throws the sound further."

Paul Martinez nodded enthusiastically. "Each design serves a different purpose, doesn't it? My Washburn is perfect for intimate venues and duet work. Your Martin has that classic parlor guitar sweetness for refined audiences.

And Thomas's Gibson can fill a concert hall."

"Exactly right," James said, carefully handing the Gibson back to its owner. "It's like having different tools for different jobs. A carpenter doesn't use the same hammer for every task."

Clara, who had been listening to the guitar discussion, stepped forward. "That's actually a perfect metaphor for what we want to talk about tonight," she said. "Different instruments serving different purposes, but all working together to create something beautiful."

The room's attention shifted to her, and Daniel felt a surge of admiration for how naturally she commanded the space.

"The Fraternal Order of Eagles," Clara continued, "is based on the idea that musicians and theater owners have different strengths, like different instruments, but we can work together to create something better than any of us could achieve alone."

She gestured toward the guitar players. "Just now, we saw three musicians sharing knowledge about their instruments, each one learning something that makes them better at their craft. That's the spirit we want to bring to the entire entertainment industry."

Marcus Reynolds stood up, his interest clearly piqued. "Miss Weston, that sounds wonderful in theory. But how does it work in practice? How do you get theater owners to see musicians as partners rather than employees?"

Daniel stepped forward, grateful for the opening. "In Seattle," he said, "we started with a simple principle: people helping people. When a musician gets sick and can't work, the Brotherhood helps support their family. When a theater faces unfair competition or hard times, the musicians rally to help."

He looked around the room, meeting the eyes of both performers and owners. "But it goes beyond just mutual aid. We've found that when everyone has a stake in everyone else's success, the quality of performances improves, audiences grow, and the whole industry benefits."

A well-dressed woman Daniel hadn't met raised her hand. "I'm Margaret Sullivan, and I own the Riverside Theater. Mr. O'Malley, what you're describing sounds like it could be expensive for theater owners. We already have tight margins."

"Mrs. Sullivan," Clara replied, "may I ask what your biggest operational challenges are?"

Margaret considered the question. "Finding reliable performers who care about the success of my theater, not just their individual paychecks. Dealing with performers who disappear when they get better offers elsewhere. Managing the constant turnover that forces me to keep training new people."

James Scott nodded knowingly. "In other words, you need performers who are invested in your theater's long-term success."

"Exactly."

"That's precisely what the Fraternal Order of Eagles provides," Daniel said. "When musicians know that their theater's success directly benefits them—not just through wages, but through profit-sharing and genuine partnership—they become invested in making that theater the best it can be."

Paul Martinez leaned forward with his Washburn guitar still in his lap. "Can you give us a specific example of how this works?"

Daniel smiled, thinking of the success stories from Seattle. "There's a theater owner named Mose Goldsmith who was one of our founding members. Before the F.O.E., he went through musicians constantly—people would work for him just long enough to get experience, then leave for better opportunities."

He paused, remembering Goldsmith's transformation. "Now, his musicians get a percentage of ticket sales when shows are successful. They help promote performances in their neighborhoods. They suggest programming that appeals to audiences they know. His theater is packed almost every night, and his musicians are making more money than they ever did just collecting wages."

"And the musicians?" asked Thomas Wright.

Clara answered. "They have job security, health support when they're sick, and a real voice in how the theater operates. Most importantly, they have the satisfaction of knowing their work is building something larger than themselves."

An older man with a violin case spoke up. "I'm Arthur Kellerman, and I've been playing in Sacramento for twenty-five years. What you're describing sounds ideal, but how do you handle disputes? What happens when musicians and owners disagree?"

Anna Morrison had prepared them for this question. "Mr. Kellerman," Daniel replied, "the Fraternal Order of Eagles has a council with equal representation from musicians and theater owners. When disagreements arise, we work toward consensus. If that's not possible, we have clear procedures for mediation."

He looked around the room. "But more importantly, we've found that when people are truly committed to the principle of people helping people, most disputes resolve themselves. It's remarkable how much conflict disappears when everyone knows that everyone else has their best interests at heart."

Marcus Reynolds stood up again. "I'm intrigued by all of this, but I have to ask—what's the commitment? If we decide to form a chapter of this organization here in Sacramento, what exactly are we signing up for?"

James Scott pulled out a folded paper from his jacket pocket. "We've brought a copy of the charter we use in Seattle. It's quite simple, really."

He began to read: "Members of the Fraternal Order of Eagles pledge to support their fellow members in times of need, to conduct their business with honesty and fairness, to treat all people with dignity and respect, and to work toward a community where people help people."

"That's it?" asked Mrs. Sullivan.

"That's it," Clara confirmed. "Everything else—the specific programs, the organizational structure, the way disputes are handled—gets worked out by the members together. The only requirement is commitment to those four principles."

Thomas Wright carefully placed his Gibson guitar back in its case. "You know," he said thoughtfully, "this reminds me of something. Different guitar makers—Martin, Washburn, Gibson—they all approach the instrument differently, but they're all trying to achieve the same thing: creating beautiful music."

He looked around the room. "Maybe that's what's been missing here in Sacramento. We've all been focused on our individual approaches—musicians trying to maximize their own success, theater owners trying to maximize their own profits—instead of recognizing that we're all trying to achieve the same thing: creating beautiful entertainment experiences."

Paul Martinez nodded enthusiastically. "And just like those guitars we were discussing, we each bring different strengths. Theater owners bring business knowledge and resources, musicians bring artistic skill and community connections."

"Combined, we could create something more powerful than any of us could achieve alone," added Arthur

Kellerman.

Margaret Sullivan had been quiet during this exchange, but now she spoke up. "I have to admit, I'm interested. The constant turnover of musicians has been exhausting, and the idea of having performers who are genuinely invested in my theater's success is appealing."

She paused, looking around at the assembled musicians. "But I need to know that this isn't just about musicians getting more benefits. I need to know there's real commitment to making the business successful."

Marcus Reynolds stood and walked to the center of the room. "Mrs. Sullivan, I think I can speak for most of the musicians here when I say we're tired of the current system too. We're tired of feeling like interchangeable parts, tired of never knowing if we'll have work next month, tired of having no voice in decisions that affect our livelihoods."

He gestured toward his fellow performers. "What these folks from Seattle are offering isn't just better working conditions. It's a chance to be partners in building something meaningful."

Daniel watched the faces around the room as Marcus spoke, and he could see the same transformation that had happened in Seattle beginning to take place. Musicians and theater owners who had entered the room as separate, often competing groups were starting to see themselves as potential partners.

"So what's the next step?" asked a theater manager Daniel hadn't met.

Clara stepped forward. "If there's genuine interest in forming a Sacramento chapter of the Fraternal Order of Eagles, we suggest starting with a small group of committed individuals—both musicians and theater owners. Work together for a few months, prove to yourselves that the principles work, then expand."

James Scott nodded. "That's exactly how Seattle started. Six theater owners and a dozen musicians meeting in a shipyard, deciding to try something new."

"And now?" asked Paul Martinez.

"Now we have over a hundred members," Daniel replied, "including not just musicians and theater owners, but music teachers, instrument makers, even some of the people who run boarding houses for performers."

Thomas Wright raised his hand. "I'd like to propose something. What if we start with the people in this room who are genuinely interested? We could meet weekly for a month, try working together on some small projects, see if the chemistry is right."

"What kind of projects?" asked Mrs. Sullivan.

Marcus Reynolds grinned. "Well, for starters, we could organize a benefit concert for the Sacramento Musicians' Relief Fund. Pool our resources—my theater provides the venue, Mrs. Sullivan provides publicity through her connections, the musicians donate their performances."

"And everyone shares in the success," added Clara. "If the concert is profitable, everyone gets a share. If someone gets sick during the preparation, everyone helps cover for them."

Arthur Kellerman nodded slowly. "A practical test of the principles before making a larger commitment. I like that approach."

One by one, the people in the room began to express their willingness to try the experiment. Musicians and theater owners, young performers and established professionals, all united by the possibility of creating something better than what they had.

As the evening wound down and people began to gather their instruments and belongings, Daniel found himself standing with the three guitar players, still discussing their instruments.

"You know what's interesting?" Thomas Wright said, cradling his Gibson. "When we started tonight, we were all focused on the differences between our guitars—Martin's traditional craftsmanship, Washburn's practical affordability, Gibson's innovative design."

"And now?" asked Paul Martinez.

"Now I'm thinking about how much better we could all sound if we played together more often," Thomas replied. "Each guitar brings something unique to the ensemble."

James Scott smiled, packing away his Martin. "That's the Fraternal Order of Eagles in a nutshell. Recognizing that our individual strengths are most powerful when they serve a common purpose."

F. Harris, one of the theater managers who had been quietly listening all evening, stepped forward. "Mr. Scott, if we're going to do this properly, we need to establish formal leadership for Sacramento's chapter. I'd like to volunteer to help with the organizational aspects."

C. F. Curry, who owned a music publishing business, nodded in agreement. "And I can help with documentation and correspondence with the Seattle chapter. I've just gotten one of those new Remington typewriters—makes everything so much more professional looking than handwritten letters."

Jake Zemansky, a violin instructor who had been intrigued by the guitar discussion, raised his hand. "I've been teaching music in Sacramento for eight years, and I'll tell you, the world is changing fast. Just last month, I took my students to see one of those new motion picture exhibitions at the Orpheum. Moving photographs! Can you imagine?"

He shook his head in amazement. "The children were fascinated, but it got me thinking—this is another form of entertainment that could either compete with musicians or give us new opportunities. What if we found ways to provide live musical accompaniment to these moving pictures?"

Thomas Wright looked up from packing his Gibson guitar. "You mean like how we play for traveling magic lantern shows?"

"Exactly!" Jake said. "The pictures move, but they're silent. They need music to tell the story, to create the right emotions. And that can only come from live musicians who can adapt to what's happening on screen."

S. Stone offered to handle financial matters, Carl Sweeney volunteered to coordinate with local theaters, and John C. March suggested he could manage communications with other potential chapters. "I've been thinking about getting one of those telephone connections installed in my office," March added. "They say you can talk directly with people in other cities now. Imagine being able to coordinate with the Seattle Eagles just by picking up a speaking device!"

Marcus Reynolds looked around at the emerging leadership structure with satisfaction. "Gentlemen, and Miss Weston, I think we have the foundation for a successful Sacramento chapter right here. And with all these new inventions—telephones, typewriters, even those moving pictures—we're going to need an organization that helps people navigate this changing world together."

As they prepared to leave the Golden Eagle Theater, Daniel reflected on how perfectly the evening had gone. The conversation about guitars had been the perfect icebreaker, allowing musicians to connect over their shared passion before moving to the larger questions of organization and cooperation. And now they had authentic local leadership emerging—F. Harris with his business management experience, C. F. Curry with his publishing connections, Jake Zemansky with his teaching expertise

Clara slipped her hand into his as they walked toward the theater's electric-lit exit. "What are you thinking?" she asked.

"I'm thinking," Daniel replied, "that Anna Morrison was right. People helping people works anywhere people are willing to try it."

Behind them, Marcus Reynolds was locking up his theater, but Daniel could see through the windows that several small groups were still talking on the sidewalk under the electric streetlights. Musicians and theater owners, continuing conversations that had started inside, beginning the relationships that would form the foundation of Sacramento's Fraternal Order of Eagles.

"Same time next week?" Marcus called out to the departing group.

A chorus of affirmative responses came back from musicians and owners alike.

"Looking forward to seeing how the Sacramento Eagles develop," someone called back.

As Daniel, Clara, and James walked back to their hotel through Sacramento's electric-lit streets, passing the occasional silent electric automobile and hearing the distant sound of music from other theaters, Daniel felt the same sense of possibility he had experienced at that first meeting in Anna Morrison's boarding house.

The Fraternal Order of Eagles was growing, expanding, adapting to new communities and new challenges. And just like the different guitar makers they had discussed—each bringing their own approach to creating beautiful instruments—each new chapter would bring its own strengths to the larger movement.

"One down," Clara said softly, squeezing his hand.

"What do you mean?"

"One successful expansion. Next stop, Folsom."

Daniel smiled, thinking about the powerhouse that sent electricity flowing twenty-two miles to light up Sacramento's streets. Soon, the Fraternal Order of Eagles would follow that same path, carrying its own form of power—the power of people helping people—from community to community until it illuminated the entire nation.

"Together," he said, echoing the word that had become their private promise to each other. "Together," Clara replied. "People helping people, one guitar at a time."

Above them, the electric lights of Sacramento continued their steady glow, proof that individual sources of strength could indeed serve entire communities. And somewhere in the distance, three different guitars were playing the same song, their unique voices blending into something more beautiful than any of them could create alone.

7

SPREADING WINGS

Railroad Circuits Across America - 1900-1904

The letter that changed everything arrived at Anna Morrison's boarding house on a rain-soaked Tuesday morning in November 1900. It was written in a shaky hand on paper that had clearly traveled far, bearing the postmark of Winnipeg, Manitoba.

"Dear Mrs. Morrison and the Seattle Eagles," it began, "My name is Margaret O'Sullivan, and I am writing from the Winnipeg General Hospital where my husband Patrick has been lying for three weeks with pneumonia. He is a fiddler with the Northern Circuit, and he was in your city last year when he heard about the Fraternal Order of Eagles..."

Anna set down her coffee and continued reading, her heart growing heavier with each line.

"Patrick came home full of stories about how your organization takes care of its members when they fall sick. How families don't go hungry when the breadwinner can't work. Mrs. Morrison, we have three small children, and I don't know how we'll pay for Patrick's medical care or put food on the table if he can't get back to performing soon. Is there any way the Eagles could help people like us, even though we're so far from Seattle? Could you tell us how to start a chapter here in Winnipeg?"

Anna folded the letter carefully and walked to the window, looking out at the bustling streets of Seattle. She placed her palm against the cool glass, feeling the slight vibration of the city's morning energy—carts rattling over cobblestones, voices calling greetings, the distant clang of the trolley bell. She took a slow breath, letting the weight of Margaret's words settle into her bones rather than simply rushing past them.

Through the window, she could see Mrs. Chen next door in her small garden plot, kneeling in the damp earth despite the drizzle, tending winter kale with patient hands. Anna watched her work—the deliberate way she pulled weeds, the gentle touch as she examined each leaf. There was a kind of prayer in it, Anna thought. The same care Margaret was showing her sick husband, the same attention Anna herself brought to each letter that arrived seeking help.

Anna stretched her arms overhead, feeling the familiar tightness in her shoulders release. So many letters. So many needs. But right now, in this moment, there was just this one—Margaret O'Sullivan in Winnipeg, waiting for an answer. Anna could give her that. One letter, one family, one act of care at a time. That was how revolutions really happened—not in grand gestures, but in the accumulation of small, mindful acts of attention.

In the two years since Daniel O'Malley and Clara Weston had successfully established Sacramento Aerie #9, similar requests had been arriving almost daily. Letters from Portland, San Francisco, Denver, Chicago, Toronto—all from performers who had heard about the Eagles from traveling musicians and wanted to bring that same spirit of mutual aid to their own communities.

"Another one?" asked Clara, entering the kitchen with her traveling coat still damp from the morning rain. She and Daniel had just returned from a three-week circuit through Oregon and Northern California, helping to establish new aeries in Portland, Eugene, and Redding.

"Winnipeg," Anna said, handing her the letter. "A fiddler's wife. Her husband is sick, they can't pay the medical bills, and they have three children."

Clara read the letter quickly, her expression growing more determined with each paragraph. "We have to help them."

"I know," Anna replied. "But it's not just them. It's dozens of communities now. Maybe hundreds. The railroad circuits are carrying news of the Eagles faster than we can possibly respond."

She moved to a large map of North America covering one wall of her kitchen, marked with pins for established aeries and letters requesting new chapters. "Look at this. In 1898, we had one aerie in Seattle. By the end of 1899, twenty. Now..." She gestured at the densely studded pins stretching from British Columbia to the Great Lakes. "Now we're getting requests from everywhere the railroad lines go."

Clara studied the map with amazement. "How many aeries do we have now?"

"One hundred and forty-seven as of last month," Anna replied. "And we've got applications pending for at least fifty more."

The door opened and Daniel entered, carrying his violin case and a bundle of mail. "Morning, Anna. Clara told me about the railroad delays—sorry we're late getting back." He kissed Clara's cheek and set down his case. "But the trip was worth it. The Redding chapter is already planning their first community benefit concert, and Portland has started a fund for musicians' medical emergencies."

"Speaking of which," Clara said, showing him Margaret O'Sullivan's letter. "Read this."

As Daniel read, Anna noticed his expression growing more serious. "We're getting these from Canada too now?"

"Two or three a week," Anna confirmed. "Vancouver, Toronto, Montreal, and now Winnipeg. The theater circuits don't stop at the border, and neither do the performers' needs."

Daniel set down the letter and looked at the map.

7 SPREADING WINGS

"Anna, this is remarkable. But it's also overwhelming. How do we possibly respond to all these requests?"

Before Anna could answer, they heard boots stomping on the back porch—the familiar rhythm of James Scott shaking off Seattle rain. He entered through the back door, his guitar case strapped across his back and his boots muddy from the streets. He'd become the Eagles' chief traveling organizer, spending most of his time on railroad circuits between San Francisco and Vancouver.

"Morning, everyone," he said, hanging his coat on the kitchen hook. "Just got back from the Canadian Pacific line. I've got news you're going to want to hear."

He pulled out a small notebook and sat at Anna's kitchen table. "I've been tracking something remarkable. People are starting aeries in towns I've never visited—they're learning the principles from traveling performers and organizing themselves."

He flipped through his notes. "I just met with a group in Calgary who started their own Eagles chapter six months ago. None of them had ever met anyone from Seattle or Sacramento. They just heard about the organization from a traveling pianist who had been helped by the Vancouver aerie when his instrument was stolen."

He turned another page. "And in Spokane, the local aerie has grown to over sixty members—not just musicians and theater owners, but shopkeepers, railroad workers, even some of the logging company supervisors. They're providing housing assistance, medical care, and job placement for anyone in the entertainment industry who needs help."

Clara shook her head in amazement. "It's like the organization is growing itself."

"That's exactly what it's doing," Anna said quietly. "We created a model for how people can take care of each other in a rapidly changing world. The same railroads carrying news of the Eagles are carrying people away from their families and home communities." She gestured toward Margaret O'Sullivan's letter. "That woman in Winnipeg—her husband travels for work, so they don't have the support of extended family when crisis strikes."

"So the Eagles are becoming their extended family," James said. "And not just for performers—for everyone who's been displaced by this new, mobile economy."

"Which explains the rapid growth," Clara added. "It's meeting a need that exists everywhere."

Anna moved to her desk and pulled out a thick folder of correspondence. "Let me show you something that's been developing over the past year." She'd been documenting how established chapters were innovating beyond their original scope.

She opened the folder and spread out letters from different aeries. "Portland Aerie #4 has established a boarding house specifically for traveling performers. Clean rooms, meals, and medical care when needed—all funded by dues and donations from local members."

She held up another letter. "San Francisco Aerie #5 has created a job placement service. When a musician arrives in town looking for work, the aerie connects them with member theaters and venues."

A third letter: "Bellingham Aerie #31 has started a medical fund that pays for everything from broken bones to childbirth expenses. No member family goes without medical care."

Daniel whistled softly. "It's not just mutual aid anymore. It's becoming a complete support system."

"And that's why people want to join," James said. "It's about knowing that you're part of a community that will take care of you no matter where your work takes you."

Anna walked back to the map. "What if this model could work for everyone?" She traced the railroad lines with her finger. "Every community with organizations dedicated to mutual aid."

Daniel picked up Margaret O'Sullivan's letter again. "So what do we do about requests like this? We can't possibly travel to every community that wants to start an aerie."

Anna moved to another desk drawer and pulled out a stack of papers. "I've been working on something. A guide—instructions for starting local aeries, organizing principles, sample bylaws, everything a community would need to establish their own chapter."

She spread the papers on the table. "The idea is to send

this packet to anyone who requests it, along with a personal letter of encouragement and an invitation to stay in touch with the Seattle headquarters."

Clara examined the documents. "This is wonderful, Anna. But how do we ensure that new aeries maintain the principles and standards of the organization?"

"We don't," Anna said simply. "At least, not by controlling them from Seattle. We do it by making sure the principles are so clear and the benefits so obvious that people will want to maintain them."

She pointed to a section of the guide. "Look here—every new aerie commits to the same basic pledge: to support fellow members in times of need, to conduct business with honesty and fairness, to treat all people with dignity and respect, and to work toward communities where people help people."

"The principles are self-reinforcing," James added. "Communities that practice genuine mutual aid prosper, and prosperous communities attract more members."

Daniel stood up and walked to the window, watching the street life of Seattle flow past. "Anna, what you're describing—this network of mutual aid organizations spreading across the continent—it could change everything."

"I think it already is," Anna replied quietly, joining him at the window.

"When you first arrived in Seattle two years ago, what

did you see?" she asked.

Daniel smiled at the memory. "Chaos. Opportunity. A city full of people chasing individual dreams without much thought for community."

"And now?"

"Now I see neighbors who look out for each other," Daniel said quietly. "A place where people help people."

Clara joined them at the window. "And if this spreads to Winnipeg, to every railroad town, we're talking about changing the entire culture."

Anna's voice grew soft. "I'm talking about honoring the people who make communities possible. The mothers who sacrifice for their children. The neighbors who help during emergencies. The workers who support each other during hard times. I'm talking about a day when the whole nation would stop to honor the people who hold communities together."

James consulted his notebook one final time. "Anna, I've got train schedules here for the next three months. Daniel, Clara, if you're willing, I think we could establish at least a dozen new aeries before the end of the year."

He looked at the map. "The Great Northern line will take us to Minneapolis, Chicago, and Detroit. The Canadian Pacific will get us to Toronto and Montreal. And the Santa Fe line could carry us down through California into Arizona and New Mexico."

Clara felt the familiar excitement of embarking on a new adventure. "What do you think, Daniel? Ready to help spread the Eagles' wings a little further?"

Daniel picked up his violin case and smiled. "I think we're not just spreading an organization anymore. We're spreading a revolution in how people take care of each other."

Anna moved to her desk and began drafting a response to Margaret O'Sullivan's letter. "Dear Mrs. O'Sullivan," she wrote, "Thank you for your letter, and please know that you and Patrick are not alone. The spirit of the Eagles reaches wherever there are people willing to help each other..."

As she wrote, the late morning sun streamed through the window, illuminating the map with its hundreds of pins representing communities where people had chosen mutual aid over isolation, cooperation over competition, and hope over despair.

Over the next three years, that map would transform in ways none of them could have imagined.

In Minneapolis, on a freezing night in March 1901, Daniel and Clara stood on a train platform at midnight, watching a newly chartered aerie present their first mutual aid check to a tubercular harmonica player. The man's wife wept as she accepted it. "We can pay the rent now," she whispered. "We can eat." By morning, news of the Minneapolis Eagles had spread to three neighboring towns, carried by the same railroad workers who had witnessed the presentation.

7 SPREADING WINGS

James Scott spent October 1902 living on trains, his guitar case serving as both instrument and portable desk. Between performances, he drafted charter applications for aeries in towns he'd never heard of—places where local performers had organized themselves after hearing stories from circuit riders. In a railroad car somewhere between Denver and Kansas City, he realized the movement was growing itself now, spreading faster than any of them could track. The revolution they'd started had taken on a life of its own.

By the summer of 1903, Anna's map had become inadequate. She'd ordered a larger one, stretching across two walls of her kitchen. Five hundred aeries, twenty-three states, four Canadian provinces. But the most remarkable pins were the ones she hadn't placed herself—the chapters started by people she'd never met, in towns she'd never visited, organized by performers and workers who'd simply heard that communities could organize to help each other. Theater owners who had initially resisted the movement were now joining when they realized that supporting their performers actually improved their businesses. Railroad workers, shopkeepers, and craftsmen started their own aeries, adapting the Eagles' principles to their own industries.

But the most significant development came from an unexpected quarter.

Frank Earle Hering, Past Worthy President of his local aerie in 1904, was not just an organizer—he was a faculty member at the University of Notre Dame, a man whose vision extended beyond helping individual communities to transforming the entire nation's understanding of care and responsibility.

Anna had corresponded with Hering several times, sharing her thoughts about how the Eagles' work honored the same principles of sacrifice and community care that mothers embodied every day. She had written to him about her dream of a day when the whole nation would stop to recognize the people who held communities together.

She had no idea he was listening so carefully.

The telegram arrived on a cold Tuesday morning in February 1904, delivered by a young man on one of the new bicycles that were becoming so popular in Seattle.

Clara and Daniel were reviewing correspondence at Anna's kitchen table when she opened it. Her hands trembled as she read, and they both looked up.

"Listen to this," she said, her voice catching. She read aloud: "F.O.E. FRANK EARLE HERING DELIVERED HISTORIC SPEECH INDIANAPOLIS FEBRUARY 7 STOP PROPOSED NATIONAL DAY TO HONOR MOTHERS STOP AUDIENCE ENTHUSIASTIC STOP MOVEMENT GAINING SUPPORT STOP TITLE: OUR MOTHERS AND THEIR IMPORTANCE IN OUR LIVES STOP YOUR COMMUNITY VISION INSPIRING NATIONAL LEADERSHIP STOP"

James, who had arrived earlier that morning, set down his coffee cup slowly. "Frank Earle Hering," he said thoughtfully. "He's not just a faculty member at the University of Notre Dame—he's a past Worthy President, and in my opinion he's going to be our Grand Worthy President before you know it! When someone of his stature speaks about honoring mothers, people listen."

Clara looked at the telegram with excitement. "Anna, this is what you've been talking about all along. Honoring the people who hold communities together."

Daniel nodded. "The Eagles started with musicians and theater owners helping each other. Now we're talking about a whole nation stopping to honor the women who make family and community possible."

A knock at the door interrupted them. Marcus Reynolds stood on the threshold, his traveling coat soaked through and his face flushed from rushing.

"Marcus!" Clara jumped up. "Come in, sit down—you look like you've run from the station."

"Practically did." He pulled off his coat and sat heavily at the table. "Did you hear about Indianapolis?"

"We just got the telegram," Clara replied.

Marcus pulled out a letter from his traveling case. "It's bigger than just one speech. Hering's got the entire F.O.E. organization behind this. They're talking about making it an official Eagles campaign—every aerie in the country working to establish a national Mother's Day." He held up the letter. "This is from Sacramento Aerie #9. They're already planning a Mother's Day celebration for this May, even though it's not official yet. The idea is spreading faster than we can track it."

Anna felt tears welling in her eyes. "Six years ago, we were just trying to help musicians pay their medical bills. Now we're part of a movement that could transform how America thinks about motherhood and community care."

Daniel picked up his violin case. "Anna, I think it's time we took another railroad journey. But this time, not just to establish new aeries—to spread word about this Mother's Day vision."

"Where would we go?" Clara asked.

James opened his railroad schedule book. "I've got contacts in Chicago, Detroit, Minneapolis, and Toronto. All cities with strong Eagles chapters, all communities that understand the principle of people helping people." He looked up at Anna. "If Hering is right, if we can get the whole nation to honor mothers one day a year, it changes everything. It makes caring for others not just a local practice, but a national value."

Anna moved to her desk and began drafting letters, but her hand paused over the first one. Margaret O'Sullivan in Winnipeg. The woman whose letter had arrived on a rain-soaked Tuesday morning four years ago.

"Dear Mrs. O'Sullivan," she wrote. "Thank you for your patience. I'm writing to tell you that the Eagles are coming to Winnipeg, and to share news that will mean more to you than I can express. Our national leadership has proposed that the entire country adopt the principle your family has been living—that communities are strongest when they honor the people who care for others. They're calling for a national Mother's Day."

She looked up at the faces around her kitchen table—Daniel, Clara, James, Marcus. All of them carried by railroad lines to places they never expected to go, all of them part of something larger than any had imagined.

Outside, a train whistle sounded, carrying someone new toward Seattle, or away from it, toward the next town where people were learning that in a rapidly changing world, the strongest communities were those where people helped people.

Anna sealed the letter and added it to the stack. She sat back in her chair, and in the sudden stillness of the kitchen, she became aware of the symphony that was always playing —had always been playing—beneath the surface of their urgent work.

From somewhere down the street, a violin sang out—Daniel , perhaps, or another musician warming up for the evening's performance. The notes rose and fell like breath itself, like waves on Puget Sound, each one connected to the last, each one making space for the next. In the parlor, she could hear Clara humming softly as she sorted correspondence, an old Irish tune that Anna's own mother had sung while kneading bread. The melody wove through the afternoon light like golden thread.

Anna closed her eyes and listened deeper. The rhythm of James's pencil scratching across paper as he planned routes and schedules—that was percussion, steady as a heartbeat. The distant train whistle, calling and answering

—that was the bass line, the foundation that carried them all. Mrs. Chen's garden shears snipping in the yard next door, the soft thud of earth being turned, the whisper of rain on leaves—all of it music, all of it connected, all of it part of one great song of people caring for people.

She thought of Margaret O'Sullivan's husband Patrick, lying in his hospital bed in Winnipeg, probably dreaming of his fiddle, of the music that had carried him across borders and through storms. She thought of every musician on every railroad line, carrying melodies from town to town like seeds, planting them in new soil. The songs connected them all—the lullabies mothers sang in Seattle and Spokane and Sacramento, the work songs that kept rhythm on the rails, the hymns that rose from churches on Sunday mornings, the dance tunes that brought communities together in celebration.

Music was the original mutual aid society, Anna realized. It asked nothing but attention. It gave everything—comfort, joy, connection, hope. It reminded them that they were not separate souls struggling alone, but notes in a larger composition, each one necessary, each one held by the others. When Patrick O'Sullivan played his fiddle in a Winnipeg dance hall, he was playing the same ancient song that Daniel played in Seattle, that Clara hummed in the kitchen, that Anna's mother had sung over the cradle—the song that said: You are not alone. You are loved. You belong.

She opened her eyes and looked at the faces around her table—Daniel, Clara, James, Marcus—and felt such a wave of gratitude it nearly took her breath away. Grateful for the railroads that had brought them together. Grateful for the music that had taught them to listen. Grateful for the mothers who had shown them what it meant to care without counting the cost. Grateful even for the hardship and need that had called them to this work, because it had revealed what was always true: that human beings were meant to help each other, to hold each other up, to make music together in the face of whatever storms might come.

Outside, the rain had stopped, and a shaft of late afternoon sunlight broke through the clouds, illuminating the map on the wall with its hundreds of pins. Each one a note. Each one a family. Each one part of the great song of connection that was spreading across the continent, carried on railroad lines and in the hearts of people who understood that love—real, practical, unglamorous love—was simply attention made visible, care made tangible, music made flesh.

By the end of 1904, there would be over 900 Eagles aeries across North America. And somewhere, on a May Sunday that was coming soon, communities across the continent would stop to honor the women who made such communities possible.

The revolution of caring had reached the halls of Notre Dame and the attention of national leaders.

But it had started here, in a Seattle kitchen, with one letter from a worried wife and the simple conviction that people could help people

THE ORDER OF GOOD THINGS

8

THE POWERHOUSE

Folsom, California - June 1904

The sound that greeted Daniel O'Malley as he stepped off the train at Folsom was unlike anything he had ever heard—a deep, rhythmic humming that seemed to emanate from the very earth itself. The American River rushed past the town with unusual force, channeled through massive concrete structures that transformed the water's power into something altogether new: electricity.

"Welcome to the source," James Scott said, shouldering his guitar case as they gathered their belongings on the platform. "Everything you saw in Sacramento—all those electric lights, those silent automobiles—it all starts here."

Clara Weston shaded her eyes against the June sun and looked toward the imposing brick structure that dominated the riverside. The Folsom Powerhouse rose from the banks of the American River like a cathedral of the industrial age, its tall smokestacks and massive generators testament to humanity's ability to harness nature's forces. Since the California Gas and Electric Company had acquired the facility around 1902, the powerhouse had become part of a growing network of hydro plants throughout the Sierra foothills, its influence extending far beyond what anyone had originally imagined.

"It's magnificent," she said softly. "And a little frightening."

Daniel understood what she meant. After five years of watching the Fraternal Order of Eagles grow from a single meeting in Seattle to chapters in multiple cities, he had developed a deep appreciation for the power of people working together. By 1904, their motto of "Liberty, Truth, Justice, and Equality" had traveled south through California, finding a new home in towns like Folsom. It was here that the values of friendship and service took root among miners, merchants, and musicians who longed for community in a restless and rapidly changing world. But this powerhouse—this was power of an entirely different magnitude.

"Gentlemen, ma'am." A voice with a slight Southern accent interrupted his thoughts. "You must be the folks from Sacramento that D.E. Wiley's been expecting."

The man approaching them was perhaps forty-five, with the bearing of someone accustomed to authority but not arrogance. He wore a simple but well-made suit, and his handshake was firm but not aggressive.

"I'm R.D. McFarland," he said. "Financial Secretary for what we hope will become Folsom's Eagles chapter. D.E.'s waiting for us at Burke's Hall—that's where we hold our meetings."

As they walked through Folsom's main street, Daniel was struck by how different this community felt from both Seattle and Sacramento. Where Seattle had been raw and urgent, and Sacramento sophisticated and established, Folsom seemed to vibrate with contained energy. The town felt prosperous but not showy, diverse but carefully ordered. He noticed several bicycles leaning against storefronts and heard the occasional ring of a telephone bell from inside businesses.

"The modern world is reaching even small towns like this," Clara observed, watching a man in a business suit emerge from a building and mount a bicycle to pedal home.

"Tell us about Folsom," Clara said to McFarland as they passed a Chinese herbalist shop next to a German bakery next to what appeared to be a Mexican cantina.

"Gold rush town, like most places around here," McFarland replied. "But we got something special when they built the powerhouse nine years ago. Then when the California Gas and Electric Company took it over a couple years back, suddenly we weren't just another played-out mining camp—we were part of something much bigger. We're lighting up California, and we were the first to bring electric power to the state prison. Can you imagine? Electric lights in a prison—that was unheard of until Folsom made it possible."

He gestured toward a group of men walking past, their clothes marked with the distinctive grime of heavy industrial work. "Powerhouse workers, mostly. Good men, hard workers. About half are Chinese, quarter Mexican, quarter various Europeans and Americans."

Daniel noticed something in McFarland's tone—respectful but careful. "Do they all work together well?"

McFarland paused before answering. "They work the same shifts, earn similar wages, face the same dangers. That creates a certain... understanding. But socially..." He shrugged. "Well, 1904 is what it is."

They turned a corner and Daniel saw Burke's Hall—a two-story wooden building with large windows and a sign advertising "Available for Meetings, Dances, and Social Functions." Through the windows, he could see perhaps twenty men gathered around tables, their conversation animated but orderly.

"That's quite a group," James observed.

"Miners, powerhouse supervisors, shopkeepers, even a couple of the railroad men," McFarland said with obvious pride. "All interested in what you folks have built up north."

As they entered Burke's Hall, Daniel was immediately approached by a tall man with prematurely gray hair and intelligent eyes that seemed to take in everything at once.

"You must be Daniel O'Malley," the man said, extending his hand. "I'm D.E. Wiley, and I've been looking forward to this conversation for months."

"Mr. Wiley, the pleasure is mine. This is Clara Weston and James Scott."

Wiley shook hands with each of them, then gestured toward the assembled group. "Gentlemen, our guests from the Fraternal Order of Eagles have arrived."

The room quieted as Daniel, Clara, and James were invited to sit at the front. Daniel surveyed the faces looking back at him—weathered miners, clean-shaven shop owners, men with the callused hands of powerhouse work, others with the ink-stained fingers of clerks and bookkeepers.

"Before we begin," Wiley said, "I think our guests should understand what we're dealing with here in Folsom. R.D., would you mind explaining our situation?"

McFarland stood and addressed the room. "Folsom's got advantages most towns don't have. We've got the powerhouse bringing in steady wages and putting us on the map. We've got the railroad connection to Sacramento. We've got enough diversity of industry that we're not dependent on any single employer."

He paused, and Daniel sensed there was more coming.

"But we've also got challenges. The powerhouse work is dangerous—we lose men to accidents more often than we'd like. The different communities in town don't always work together as well as they could. And frankly, some of the benefits of our prosperity aren't shared as fairly as they might be."

A man near the back raised his hand. "What R.D.'s trying to say politely is that the Chinese and Mexican workers do most of the dangerous jobs at the powerhouse, but they don't get promoted to supervisor positions, and they're not welcome in most of the town's social organizations."

Wiley nodded gravely. "That's correct, unfortunately. It's one of the reasons we're interested in the Fraternal Order of Eagles. We're hoping to find ways to build stronger community connections across some of these... divisions."

Clara leaned forward. "Mr. Wiley, can you be more specific about what you're hoping to achieve?"

Wiley considered the question carefully. "Miss Weston, I'll be direct with you. The F.O.E., as I understand it, is designed to help people support each other regardless of their economic position—musicians and theater owners working together, for instance."

"That's correct."

"What we're wondering is whether that principle could apply to other kinds of differences as well. Not full integration—I'm not naive about what's possible in 1904—but perhaps more cooperation, more mutual respect."

Daniel felt a complex mix of emotions. On one hand, he was encouraged by Wiley's obvious concern for all of Folsom's residents. On the other hand, he was painfully aware that the Fraternal Order of Eagles, like most fraternal organizations, had membership restrictions that would exclude many of the people Wiley was concerned about.

"Mr. Wiley," he said carefully, "I appreciate your vision. The principle of people helping people doesn't recognize economic or cultural boundaries. But I need to be honest with you about the practical limitations we face as the Fraternal Order of Eagles."

He looked around the room. "The F.O.E. follows the membership standards of most fraternal organizations of our time. That means..." He paused, choosing his words carefully. "That means our formal membership is restricted to men of Caucasian background."

The room fell silent. Daniel could see disappointment on several faces, but also understanding—this was not news to these men.

"However," Clara said, stepping into the silence, "that doesn't mean the principles of the Fraternal Order of Eagles can't benefit the entire community."

She stood and moved to the center of the room. "In Seattle, we've found ways to extend the benefits of mutual aid and cooperation beyond formal membership. Chinese merchants who support our musicians during hard times. Mexican railroad workers who help promote our concerts. Everyone benefits when the community prospers."

James Scott nodded and added, "The formal organization might have restrictions, but the spirit of people helping people that drives the Fraternal Order of Eagles doesn't have to."

Wiley looked around the room at his fellow townspeople. "Gentlemen, what are your thoughts?"

An older man with the bearing of a mine foreman spoke up. "I've been watching this town for fifteen years, and I'll tell you what I see. The powerhouse workers—Chinese, Mexican, German, American—they help each other out when there's an accident, when someone gets hurt. They don't worry about paperwork or formal membership. They just do what needs doing."

"That's exactly right," said another man. "My shop serves everyone in town, and everyone's money spends the same. When the Chinese New Year celebration needed a place to hold their banquet, we made it work. When the Mexican families needed help after the flood last year, the whole town pitched in."

McFarland stood again. "What I'm hearing is that we already practice a lot of the principles of the F.O.E. informally. The question is whether we can make it more systematic, more reliable."

Daniel felt a spark of inspiration. "Mr. McFarland, what if we approached this differently? What if we formed an official Folsom chapter of the Fraternal Order of Eagles with membership following the standard requirements, but we also established formal partnerships with other community organizations?"

"What do you mean?" asked Wiley.

"I mean," Daniel said, warming to the idea, "what if the Folsom Eagles worked directly with the Chinese

Benevolent Association, the Mexican Mutual Aid Society, whatever organizations the other communities have? Not combined membership, but coordinated mutual aid."

Clara's eyes lit up with understanding. "When the Eagles organize a benefit concert, the Chinese musicians could participate as honored guests, not members. When there's a community emergency, all the organizations could coordinate their response."

James nodded enthusiastically. "I've seen similar arrangements in other towns. It's not perfect, but it's better than completely separate communities."

Wiley looked intrigued. "That would be... unprecedented, as far as I know. But it might work."

A younger man near the front raised his hand. "I work at the powerhouse with Chinese and Mexican men every day. We trust each other with our lives down in those generator rooms. It would be good to find a way to extend that trust into the rest of community life."

Another man added, "My wife teaches at the school, and she says the Chinese children are some of the smartest, most dedicated students she's ever had. Their families value education, hard work, community support—all the same things we Eagles say we value."

A third man, who Daniel noticed had ink stains on his fingers suggesting clerical work, spoke up. "I've been thinking about this changing world we're living in. Just last week, I saw my first moving picture exhibition when a traveling showman came through town. And I've heard they're planning to install telephone service here next year, connect us directly to Sacramento."

He paused, looking around the room. "But here's something interesting—I also heard one of those new phonograph cylinders by a fellow named Len Spencer. He's been recording since 1888, and his ragtime recordings are something else entirely. What struck me is that he's found a way to capture the energy and spirit of that music, even though he's not from that tradition himself. Yet I've heard that even black listeners appreciate his recordings."

The man leaned forward with growing excitement. "All these new inventions—motion pictures, telephones, phonographs, those typewriting machines they use in the big city offices—they're changing how people work and live. But they can also isolate people if we're not careful. Maybe that's another reason why we need organizations like the Eagles—to make sure that progress brings people together instead of driving them apart."

Daniel could see the energy in the room shifting as the men began to imagine possibilities rather than focusing on limitations.

"So here's what I propose," Wiley said, standing at the front of the room. "We form Folsom Aerie 929 of the Fraternal Order of Eagles, following the standard membership requirements. But we also reach out to the other community organizations and propose a formal alliance for mutual aid and community support."

"What would that look like practically?" asked

McFarland.

"Well," Wiley said thoughtfully, "when there's an accident at the powerhouse, all the organizations contribute to supporting the injured worker's family, regardless of which community he comes from. When there's a celebration or festival, we Eagles coordinate to make sure everyone benefits from the increased business and activity."

Clara stood up. "Mr. Wiley, that's exactly the kind of thinking that makes the Fraternal Order of Eagles successful. You're finding ways to extend the principles beyond the limitations of the formal structure."

Daniel felt a surge of admiration for both Wiley and the assembled men. They were wrestling honestly with the constraints of their time while still trying to build something better.

"Gentlemen," he said, "would you be willing to try this experiment? Form an official Eagles chapter while also reaching out to build bridges with the other communities? And I should mention—we Eagles have a motto that guides us in all our interactions: 'If I cannot speak well of an Eagle, I will not speak ill of him.' This principle of avoiding gossip and criticism extends naturally to how we treat all our neighbors, whether they're formal members or not."

Wiley looked around the room. "All in favor?"

Every hand in the room went up.

"Then let's make it official," Wiley said. "R.D., do you

have the charter paperwork?"

As McFarland began distributing papers and the men of Burke's Hall prepared to formally establish Folsom Aerie 929, Daniel found himself thinking about the powerhouse humming just outside the building. Like that massive facility, the Fraternal Order of Eagles was learning to harness different forms of energy—economic cooperation, cultural appreciation, community support—and channel them toward a common purpose.

It wasn't perfect. The formal membership restrictions were a painful reminder of the limitations of their era. But within those constraints, these men were finding ways to build something better, something that honored the dignity and contributions of all their neighbors.

After the charter paperwork was completed and Wiley had been elected as the first president of Aerie 929, the new Eagles began discussing their first collaborative project.

"The Chinese community is planning a celebration for the completion of their new temple next month," said one of the powerhouse supervisors. "What if we offered to help with security and logistics, and they invited the whole town to attend? We could even arrange for one of those new motion picture cameramen to document it—I heard there's a fellow with a moving picture machine coming through the valley this summer."

"And the Mexican families have been talking about organizing a festival around the Day of the Dead in November," added another man. "Maybe we could help with that too. With bicycles becoming so popular, we could organize delivery of supplies and help coordinate between all the neighborhoods."

James Scott smiled as he listened to the planning. "This is exactly how it started in Seattle," he said to Daniel and Clara quietly. "One project at a time, one relationship at a time, until the whole community was stronger."

As the meeting broke up and the men of Folsom's newest Eagles chapter began to head home, Daniel stepped outside Burke's Hall to listen to the sound of the powerhouse. The deep, steady humming continued, sending electricity twenty-two miles south to light up Sacramento's streets and power its electric automobiles.

"What are you thinking?" Clara asked, joining him on the steps.

"I'm thinking," Daniel said, "that Anna Morrison was right about everything. People helping people is the most powerful force in the world. Even when we can't do it perfectly, even when we're constrained by the prejudices of our time, the impulse to help each other is what makes communities strong."

Clara slipped her hand into his. "And I'm thinking that we've just witnessed something remarkable. Men choosing to work within the system to expand it, rather than just accepting its limitations."

They stood together in the gathering dusk, listening to the sound of the powerhouse and watching the first electric lights come on in the windows of Folsom's diverse neighborhoods. Chinese lanterns glowed red in one section of town, Mexican cantinas echoed with guitar music in another, and the lights of German and Irish and American families twinkled throughout the community.

It wasn't the integrated society that future generations would build. But it was a beginning—a recognition that the principle of people helping people was stronger than the barriers that divided them.

"Come on," James said, appearing in the doorway behind them. "D.E. Wiley wants to take us to dinner at the Chinese restaurant. Says it's the best food in town, and he wants to thank the owner for supporting the powerhouse workers during the strike last year."

As they walked through Folsom's streets toward a meal that would bring together the formal leaders of the new Eagles chapter and the informal leaders of the Chinese community, Daniel reflected on how much the Fraternal Order of Eagles had grown and changed since that first meeting in Seattle six years ago.

What had started as a solution to a musicians' strike had become something much larger—a way of thinking about community that transcended individual prejudices and formal limitations. It wasn't perfect, but it was progress.

And in the distance, the powerhouse continued its steady work, proving that when different sources of energy were properly harnessed and coordinated, they could illuminate entire regions. There had been an energy source emanating from Folsom since the powerhouse went online, and what had expanded in the area since could only be described as a continued flow of progress and community bliss.

Just like people helping people, one community at a time.

ABOUT THE AUTHOR

James M. Fox is a retired IT professional and musician. He recently learned about the Fraternal Order of Eagles through an open mic hosted in Folsom and was so impressed by the story of how the Eagles formed in 1898 to settle a musician strike, that he became a member and was inspired to create this book. The fact that this organization is all about People Helping People, the force behind Mother's Day and Social Security, really excited him to learn more. For more information please visit foxfarmstudios.com and theorderofgoodthings.com.

www.ingramcontent.com/pod-product-compliance
Lightning Source LLC
LaVergne TN
LVHW041609070526
838199LV00052B/3048